SIDETRACKED
BY MEDIOCRATES

AN ALLEGORY ABOUT REAL SUCCESS

BILL PALMER

Little Frog PUBLISHING

Little Frog Publishing
Southside, Alabama
www.facebook.com/LittleFrogPublishing

This book is a work of fiction. Names, characters, places, and incidents are the
product of the author's imagination or are used fictitiously, and any resemblance
to actual events or locales or persons, living or dead, is entirely coincidental.

ISBN 978-0-9994251-0-7 (Paperback Edition)

Printed in the United States of America

Book design by Rennie Palmer

Dedicated to the glory
of the Great God

ACKNOWLEDGMENTS

Writing a book—even a short one such as the one in your hands—is no easy affair. Two of the greatest challenges facing a writer are keeping the reader in mind and staying on task. Family, friends, and coworkers who agreed to review all or part of my book helped me with both.

The first challenge, keeping the reader in mind, becomes difficult because of a great irony for writers—*the creative mind can be inflexible!* Creative people see beauty in what they create, which is why we create. The problem for us is that we do not always consider how elusive that beauty is to others. The different points of view offered by my "reviewers" were invaluable to me as I labored for mastery of this allegory.

The second challenge has been the toughest for me. In pursuing high standards, I tend to turn my passions into chores. In short, perfectionism becomes procrastination! Consequently, I profited immensely from the occasional "kick-in-the-pants" that came every time someone asked me about my progress.

Sidetracked by Mediocrates is better because of my friends, coworkers, and family. I offer my sincere thanks to all of you!

It is my wife to whom I owe my greatest debt. She designed the cover, drew the illustrations, and laid out the book. She also took care of many of the chores associated with independent publishing. Her greatest contribution, however, was her willingness to listen patiently as I excitedly read each newly completed page, quite often subjecting her to second or third readings of the preceding pages for context! Thank you Baby!

I also owe a debt of gratitude to my brother, Bob Palmer, who spoke with me on numerous occasions about my book, starting in the idea stage and ending with recommended edits on the manuscript I sent him. One of his suggestions that found its way into the story is the use of the Socratic Method. (Mediocrates, of course, applies it in a half-hearted way. What else would you expect?)

Thanks go to my sisters, Claire Ferguson and Coralie Maples, who read through the manuscript version. Each of them made the story a bit better with their thoughtful edits.

My mother-in-law, Sofie Banham, surprised me with her meticulous approach to my allegory, though I shouldn't have been surprised. She never does anything half-heartedly. Thanks, Sofie, for taking such care, as you always do!

Thanks also to my brother-in-law, Lesz Banham, for reading my manuscript. He's a busy man, and I got the manuscript to him quite late, but he still managed to read it and tell me his impressions.

Ken Riddle, a friend from high school, proved to be an important asset in the editing process. Ken is an architect, and so I asked him to take a look at what I had written regarding the two bridges Nikos built. Thanks, Ken, for your insight.

My friend Dennis Cartwright, who shares with me a passion for coffee, came over to my house on a couple of occasions to talk over my book. Thanks, Dennis, for your input!

Several of my co-workers sacrificed their time to read and comment on my story. Linda Naselli and Lori Ewell each met with me on more than one occasion, pointing out potential problems in the text. Thanks!

Nick Amsden, Sarah Garcia, and Barbi Heilker, also co-workers, met with me for lunch one day to discuss the book. I profited immensely from our little round-table discussion. Thanks!

Thanks also to Andy Burnett, Ed Coleman, Tammy Foster, Steve Moody, Gary and Kim Petty, and David Treybig, for reading and commenting on my story.

I appreciated all of the comments, edits, and suggestions of family, friends, and co-workers.

CONTENTS

INTRODUCTION

As a writer and editor, I love words and their power, and I love to play with words. It was a playful moment in my mind that sparked this allegory. I was considering the word "mediocrity" not long after having read or heard the names of Greek philosophers. It dawned on me rather suddenly that *Mediocrates* would serve as a wonderful name for a fanciful philosopher whose life is dedicated to the middle of the road.

But what would be the venue for serving up this whimsical pun?

I decided to create an allegory about success in life. Every bookstore in America offers self-help books to an insatiable public feverishly seeking an easy way to success. Regrettably, many people equate success with an advance in status or an increase in material wealth. At the same time, compromises in quality have become ubiquitous. It seems that everywhere we look Americans are settling—settling for mediocrity in their work, mediocrity in their schools, and mediocrity in their family lives.

We desperately need guidance toward genuine success. This allegory is an inverse look at the search for success, which I believe to be part-and-parcel with the search for excellence. Genuine excellence, however, does not exist in a vacuum; it appears only in the context of relationships. This concept is the premise for *Sidetracked by Mediocrates*.

In substance and style, the book in your hands owes a debt to other works. Chief among them in terms of substance is *The Seven Laws of Success*, a booklet written and published by Herbert W. Armstrong in 1961. My allegory is not intended to provide an exhaustive list of character traits necessary for success. As such, it draws from *The Seven Laws of Success*, but does not duplicate the list of laws precisely.

Two other works influenced the style I have adopted: *The Great Divorce*, an allegory C.S. Lewis published in 1945, and *The Richest Man in Babylon*, a series of personal finance parables first published in book form in 1926 by George Samuel Clason. Both these books, as well as mine, are fantasy, yet the chief concern of each is discovering truth we can use in our lives. My hope is that *Sidetracked by Mediocrates* will accomplish this objective—helping you explore the truth about success, but doing so in a fantastic setting.

As you read this allegory, you will quickly realize that I have given my characters, and even my town, Greek names. The clothing and some of the customs also reflect the ancient Greek world. I infused my story with a Greek feel because the Western World looks to the ancient Greeks as the birthplace of philosophy, and Mediocrates is a philosopher. However, my purpose is not historical, but creative. I did not intend to reproduce an accurate facsimile of the ancient Greek world, but merely to suggest such as a venue for a young man's search for success.

I also ask the reader to keep in mind that I do not advocate the teachings of my fictional guru, Mediocrates. In the story you are about to read, he's an anti-hero, the obstacle to true success. It's up to you to negotiate your way through his lies to truth, and to real success!

Bill Palmer
Round Rock, Texas
September 2017

CHAPTER I

THE QUESTION

T he brisk wind opposed his every labored step up the mountain and his ears were already aching with the chill. Nikos was sure his feet would be swollen before he reached the top. He began to doubt himself, wondering whether he had been a fool to seek the legendary Hypatos. Some of his fellow townsfolk insisted they had seen the old philosopher, but most believed him to be nothing more than a fireside fabrication.

Even so, Nikos pressed on with the hope of finding out for himself, secretly nursing an ambition to become a disciple—if the old man truly existed! After all, the individuals who believed in Hypatos were some of his town's most respected citizens. One was Alexandros, the merchant whose luck in stocking the right inventory at just the right time was a source of wonder and envy among Pouthena's other merchants. Another was Andreas, renowned for his skill at consistently bringing in the best tuna and sea bass every day.

A third was Penelope, whom Nikos had known and loved since he was a toddler sitting on her knee. She had an uncanny knack for weaving robes, sashes, and tunics that both pleased the eye and endured the roughest conditions. It was Penelope who had ignited within Nikos the desire to "climb the mountain," as she would say.

And then there was Melissa. A broad smile crossed the young man's face as he considered his long-time friend. Though he had known her as long as he could remember, he had recently begun to feel something stronger.

Up to this point in his trek, Nikos had been fighting only the wind, but now the trail joined forces with his blustery enemy. Narrowing to a few inches, the track attacked his feet with rocks and ruts and roots, each taking turn against beleaguered sandals. The slope had become progressively steeper, transforming his hike into a strenuous climb.

Less than an hour of this torment had passed when Nikos was confronted by an even more troubling sight in the distance. The mountain itself seemed to rise up on the left side of the trail, even as the earth on the right plunged. He would soon be hugging the rock wall to avoid the perilous drop. Nikos paused, impulsively surrendering to his growing dread.

"Ho there, young man!"

The words thrust themselves into his consciousness, momentarily displacing apprehension. Nikos turned to see an old man sitting not far from the trail. His hair and beard were a bit unkempt, the victims of this stiff mountain breeze. The old man's robe professed only moderate quality. Although it was relatively clean, the robe featured several prominent wrinkles in the fabric that competed with its pleats. Apparently, the man before him did not place great value on appearance.

Surely this odd individual was not Hypatos, whose dress and demeanor was said to betray a consuming passion for excellence in every aspect of life. Besides, Hypatos purportedly lived at the summit—Nikos was only halfway up the mountain. Without any real enthusiasm, he took a few tentative steps toward the peculiar character. As he did, the man labored for a moment to stand, but quickly abandoned his plan and slumped back onto a stump that served as his perch.

"What brings you here?" he queried.

"I'm headed to the top to find Hypatos," Nikos replied, sheepishly admitting to a purpose that might be viewed as foolish. A handful of his fellow townsfolk had ridiculed Nikos when he spoke of making this climb, leaving him with a desire to keep his aspirations to himself.

"I'm Nikos, from Pouthena," he resumed, then quickly added his own question in hopes of changing the subject. "And who are you?"

"Not so fast, Nikos from Pouthena," the old man chided, his tone conveying a trace of assumed authority. "First tell me why you're making such a difficult climb."

Nikos squirmed, not at all enjoying this encounter. He had left Pouthena in a momentary burst of energy and enthusiasm, never fully considering exactly what he hoped to accomplish. True, he wanted to meet Hypatos, and true, he wanted to be a disciple. But why? He knew Penelope and Alexandros and half a dozen others who claimed to have met him. He knew they credited Hypatos with teaching them what they needed for success.

"I want to be a success in life!" Nikos blurted out, hoping his earnestness would be enough to end the questioning.

"And what does success mean to you?" the annoying old man continued, speaking with a bizarre blend of authority and disinterest.

Nikos wasn't expecting the question. On the surface, it was simple enough, but not so easy to answer, especially since he had never really thought deeply about what success meant. Of course, he had dreamed of reclining before sumptuous feasts, of merely clapping his hands to summon servants, and of popular acclaim among his fellow townsfolk. It wasn't until this moment that these images were unmasked as pretenders. None could claim to be more than a consequence of success. So what would success be for him?

"I'm waiting," the old man prompted. A hint of judgment resided in those aged eyes.

"I don't know," Nikos admitted. "But when I find Hypatos, he'll teach me," he added in a mildly defiant and self-assertive retort.

"Mediocrates," the old man said, this time in a more conciliatory manner.

"What?" Nikos responded. Then, with a flash of realization, "Oh, that's your name!"

"Come sit with me," Mediocrates intoned, "and I'll help you on your way."

Nikos considered the invitation, glancing back at the treacherous conditions of the trail. Perhaps it would be wise to accept the help of this old man in spite of his gruff temperament. After all, he undoubtedly knew this mountain well. Besides, the longer Nikos lingered here, the more intimidating the trek appeared. He decided he needed the assistance of Mediocrates.

"Thank you," Nikos offered, sitting on a grassy spot at the old man's feet. "Is there an easier way to the top?"

Mediocrates laughed. It wasn't the timid, unassuming laugh of the fearful, but neither was it the robust laugh of the bold and adventurous. The laugh came across as measured, or even calculating. It left Nikos perplexed.

"If you insist on reaching the summit, there is no easy way,"

Mediocrates advised. The sentence trailed off, as though to suggest something was left unsaid. The ambiguity was too much for Nikos to leave untested.

"What other choice do I have?" he asked, oblivious to the trap he had entered.

"Why, you have the choice of life," the old philosopher responded, smug satisfaction lying just below his mask of astonishment. "You can choose to struggle up that path to an uncertain future; no, rather a future *certain* to be filled with horrors and impediments along the way, yet uncertain in outcome."

Nikos felt his resolve ebbing. It was as though the old man had struck him in the gut. The young man had left Pouthena before sunrise, hoping to avoid the stares and glares of fellow residents, hoping not to have his mind challenged. He had avoided confrontation then, but now it stood before him in the guise of a withered old man in wrinkled robes. Now Nikos faced an uncomfortable truth and a disheartening choice. Life and safety and comfort, or danger and toil—and possibly even injury or death.

"Why the long face, Nikos? What is it that drove you here?"

"I want to succeed!" an exasperated young man exclaimed, almost as if to bolster his own resolve. "I want to be a success in life!"

"Tell me," Mediocrates asked, "what do you imagine success in life to be?"

That again! Nikos bristled at the human bulldog before him. What gall to persist in this line of questioning! Yet Nikos could not block the growing unease he felt at his own folly for departing on this quest with the flimsiest notion of his goals. He was also angry, and it was that anger that prompted his next tactic. He would ask a retaliatory question. He would turn the tables on the old man.

"I've already told you I don't know. I was on the way to learn from Hypatos, but now you're here. So I'll ask you! What is success, and how can I have it?"

A subtle smile crossed the lips of the old philosopher. He was pleased that he had brought this young man to a moment of choice so quickly.

"Success is not easy to define," Mediocrates began. The young man took his turn at being smug, but the moment did not last. "Each of us must decide for ourselves. There is a critical question that we must ask ourselves first, but the so-called disciples of Hypatos never do."

Mediocrates stopped, allowing an awful silence to envelope Nikos. The old man leaned forward almost imperceptibly, slightly bowing his head as if to add gravity to his enigmatic statement. Nikos waited, but the philosopher did not move. Finally, the young man could wait no longer.

"What is that question?"

Looking up in feigned surprise, Mediocrates studied the youth seated before him. Yes, now was the time to alter the course of Nikos.

"The question you must ask yourself is this: 'Are you willing to throw away all of your todays for a tomorrow that may never come?'" The grizzled philosopher, sitting on a tree stump with Nikos at his feet, stared into the eyes and heart and soul of the young man.

It was a big question, and one worth considering. Nikos knew then that he would not be climbing any higher. Mediocrates would be his teacher.

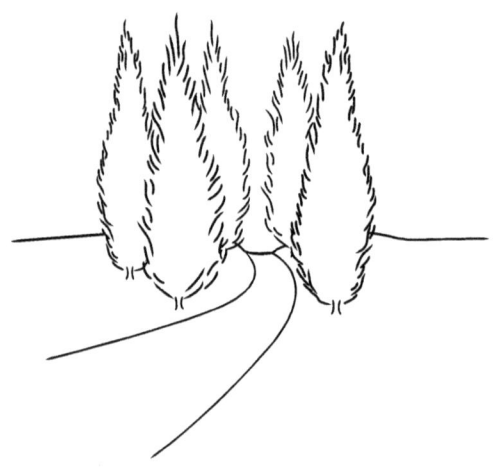

CHAPTER 2

THE
RETURN

Following the trail around a particularly thick cluster of juniper trees, Nikos suddenly found himself greeted by a familiar vista of Pouthena. Pausing, he recalled unbridled boyhood days spent playing in this grassy field boxed in by the mountain behind and the sea-side town before him. Now, seeing the white-washed homes clustered along narrow, zigzagging streets, he felt a quiet joy. He was home!

Funny, he thought, turning to look again at the junipers. Those very trees had been an important element in so many imagined adventures, and yet he had failed to recognize them from the far side. Until this trek up the mountain, Nikos had never gone beyond them. They had been silent sentinels watching over the boundary between known and unknown. Nikos smiled, happy at the thought that he had set aside childhood boundaries.

Eager to share the day's events with someone—anyone— Nikos headed to the Square. The sun was still an hour from setting, but the "returning hero" was sure to find a few of his friends already there, wresting a day-end morsel of joy from an otherwise routine day.

It was the resonant voice of Stefanos he heard first. Nikos had always admired his popular friend, a young man two years his senior. With the strength of the Minotaur and the cleverness of Apollo, Stefanos intimidated most of the town's young men, including Nikos at times. Today would be different, Nikos thought. Today he would captivate everyone with his daring trek up the mountain.

"Here he is now," Stefanos bellowed with a mischievous grin. "We were wondering where you've been today."

Nikos couldn't have imagined a better opportunity to begin his tale. What luck!

"I've climbed the mountain," he said, waiting a moment to punctuate his terse statement. Stefanos straightened a bit, exchanging his comfortable slouch for a more earnest posture. Once Nikos was sure all his friends had grasped the magnitude of those four words, he continued. "I went to find Hypatos."

"Did you find him?" a wide-eyed boy asked in wonder. He was one of four tag-alongs listening intently to the older boys.

"Of course he didn't," Stefanos laughed. "Hypatos is no more real than Zeus or Poseidon." Then, turning to Nikos and speaking matter-of-factly, he simply said "Go on." Nikos hesitated, no longer sure of the reaction to his little expedition. Faced with unmitigated silence, he braced himself and continued.

"I left before sunrise to beat the heat," he lied, remembering now that he had purposely snuck out in darkness to avoid ridicule. How thoughtless he was to forget. How stupid to volunteer this tale. And how foolish to tell it in the Square!

"I'd have come home in the dark, too!" Lykos howled. This young man was not someone Nikos liked much. In fact, he wasn't very popular with anyone. He didn't say much and rarely joined in any fun, but he was always there, lurking at the fringe of conversations, ready to pounce at any vulnerability. When he did speak, it was usually to ridicule, and usually abrupt. A predatory sneer silently took up residence on his face, conveying the contempt he felt toward Nikos, and everyone else, for that matter.

"That's enough," Stefanos interjected. "Go on, Nikos."

"I knew when I left that Hypatos might not exist," he said defensively. "But I had to find out for myself. Besides, I don't know how many times Penelope has told me about the first time she climbed the mountain. She was a young woman, and she insists that meeting Hypatos changed her life."

There was almost a reverence to his words when Nikos spoke about Penelope. His own mother and father had died in the *year of dying*—the year when pestilence ravaged Pouthena. No memories of his real parents vied with those of the doting woman who gave him a home. As far as he was concerned, she was his mother. And her claim that she had met Hypatos was good enough to inspire Nikos to make his own trek.

"Well, did you meet him?" Stefanos asked politely.

"Not exactly," Nikos replied. "I stopped half-way, right at a point when the trail becomes almost impossible. That's when I met Mediocrates."

Nikos wasn't prepared for what happened next.

"That old scoundrel is still around?" Stefanos asked, barely hiding his pleasure in revealing a long-held secret.

"You've met him?" Nikos asked, unable to hide his shattered pride. "When?"

"A couple of years ago. Do you remember all those times I was late to our evening gatherings?"

Nikos stood silent, not sure what had happened. He had launched into his tale fully expecting attentive ears and watchful eyes among his collection of friends. He had expected at least some admiration, perhaps even envy, as he regaled the cluster of young men assembled for a night of cold ale and one-upmanship. But not this!

"I made half a dozen trips up that mountain," Stefanos stated soberly. "Never once did I see or learn anything of value. And that old man—he's nothing but a faker," he added, spitting the last word out as though settling a score.

The group remained focused on Stefanos, though he now seemed lost in some unpleasant memories, judging from the sour look on his face. Nikos looked around, perturbed at the outcome and miffed at his friend. He, too, was lost in silence, though he wore a blend of bewilderment and defeat on his face.

"Tell us great things," Lykos snickered, taking the void in conversation as an invitation. "Tell us about your heroic journey. Tell us how you conquered ant hills and dazzled furry little creatures with your exploits. Tell us, tell us, tell us," he demanded, still wearing an obnoxious sneer.

Nikos turned and walked away, never responding. As he left the Square, he could hear laughter echoing off the masonry buildings surrounding Pouthena's heart. He could almost feel eyes fixed on his form as he disappeared into the distance.

Shadows had grown long by the time the tiny cottage came into view. It was a safe place, a haven from the disappointments of life. Smoke rising from the kitchen's chimney let Nikos know that Penelope had started dinner. More than that, it conveyed a warmth he sorely needed now. He longed for the simple pleasure of sitting at dinner, chatting easily about unimportant things.

"You've had a big day," Penelope said from the door, more as a question than an observation. "You left before I could fix you breakfast." Her eyes, filled with a mother's acceptance, were bright and cheerful, yet uncompromising. There was no mistaking her love for this young man she had raised, but neither was there any mistaking a firm resolve veiled behind her eyes. She expected an explanation.

"I've climbed the mountain," Nikos said, remembering the unforeseen sequence of events those words had touched off in the Square an hour earlier. He paused, looking into Penelope's eyes to gauge her response.

"And what did you find?" she inquired. The words, issued without a hint of emotion, frustrated Nikos. Penelope had often encouraged him to climb the mountain, especially now that he had reached manhood. Today her words were flat and passionless. Why?

"How far did you climb?" she asked, breaking into his thoughts. This time the question cut, as though she already knew he stopped halfway up the mountain.

Suddenly a bit embarrassed, Nikos scrambled for the right words. "An old man stopped me," he explained. "I knew you wouldn't want me to be rude, so I left the trail to see what he wanted." Even as he spoke the words, Nikos thought of past excuses he had made and how little they mattered to Penelope. Again he peered into her eyes in an attempt to read her thoughts.

"So, what did he want?" she said, uttering the five words much as Demos, the town's magistrate, might. Nothing Nikos had ever tried could prevail against her questions, or her scrutiny, once she set her will to discover the truth.

"He asked me why I was climbing the mountain," the young man explained, head down. "In fact, he asked more than once.

His persistence annoyed me."

"What did you tell him?" Penelope pressed.

That question, again! Is the reason for the climb that important, Nikos wondered.

"I told him I want to succeed in life." He uttered the sentence reluctantly, as though paying tribute rather than seeking victory.

"Do you?" Penelope asked, speaking tenderly. The words were gentle, but resolute.

"Yes," Nikos declared defensively. "Mediocrates—that's the old man's name—has agreed to help me."

Penelope's eyes changed ever so slightly when Nikos mentioned Mediocrates by name. Could it be that she, too, had met this old man?

"Do you know him?" he asked.

"Better than I'd like to," she admitted. Nikos caught a glimpse of something more in her eyes, but he could not tell what. "And that certainly is not the point. How do you think Mediocrates can help you?"

At first the young man wasn't sure how to respond, but then he remembered the last question the old philosopher had asked him. It was that question that convinced him not to climb any higher. It was that question that would justify him now.

"Well, to begin with, he told me about an important question the disciples of Hypatos never ask themselves," Nikos explained with some satisfaction. His satisfaction was short-lived.

"You mean the question about whether you're willing to throw away all your todays for a tomorrow that may never come?" Penelope challenged.

Nikos was stunned. He could not imagine Penelope stopping halfway up the mountain to speak with Mediocrates as he had. Few people in town could match her fire, and fewer ever attempted to stand in her way when she set her mind to a task.

"How, exactly, are you throwing away all your todays?" she demanded, recognizing in his silence that she had identified the right question. Standing in the door, Penelope waited, her white hair neatly framing a countenance worthy of consideration. It was the waiting that Nikos hated. It forced him to think, and it forced him to confront his assumptions.

"If I worked for Alexandros again, as I did last year, rising early every morning to help him prepare for trading days, what would I have to show for it?" Nikos replied plaintively. "I'm throwing away my days, and he's the one who lives well!"

"Nikos, my child," Penelope said, the tone of her voice conveying the same tenderness as her hand, which touched his upper arm affectionately. "Neither today nor tomorrow is about riches, or fame, or even great accomplishments. Each day is a gift. What matters most is how we use that gift. Think about that."

CHAPTER 3

ON THE STEPS

The morning's bitterly cold fingers explored the surface of the young man's clothing, seeking some unguarded access to the heat of his body. Drawing the cloak around himself tightly, Nikos trudged up the trail, thankful for the garment's quality.

Penelope had stayed up late practically every night for a month working on it, at times even reworking portions that weren't quite right in her eyes. Nikos could never see why, sometimes joking that she was seeing things that weren't there, or perhaps suggesting she could not sleep. Penelope simply continued working, undaunted by his good-natured teasing.

Nikos was surprised, and a little embarrassed, when she gave him the cloak. The extra effort had been for him. At the time, all she said was, "You'll need this." Both knew why. Both knew he would soon head back up the mountain, though neither spoke about the impending journey.

A particularly sharp stabbing pain in his right foot wrenched Nikos from his reverie. Lifting his foot to examine his sandal, he saw the culprit. The rock was no bigger than an almond, but an exceptionally jagged edge made this little soldier a real threat. Nikos extracted it from the sole of his sandal, tossing the invader into a nearby thicket of trees.

That enemy had been part of the same battalion of exposed roots and loose rocks that had attacked his feet on the previous trek. This time Nikos smiled, knowing he was drawing close to the spot where he first encountered Mediocrates. Hopefully, the old man could still be found.

Nikos paused a moment, looking up. No clouds populated the crisp blue sky, as though the frigid temperatures had convinced them not to venture from their dens and lairs. Now that the crunching of his sandals against rocks and roots could no longer be heard, he found himself in the stillness. The moment, though cold, was beautiful and powerful.

Shattering the quiet, the voice of Mediocrates called out to Nikos. "You've returned," he said, yawning as he did. "Why?"

Nikos was taken aback by the philosopher's casual and dismissive attitude. The old man was seated on what appeared to be steps carved into the side of a granite slope. He was wearing the same wrinkled robe, though it was now partially covered by some sort of roughly-prepared animal skin.

"To begin my lessons," Nikos responded, a bit irritated that Mediocrates should show so little interest in their new teacher-disciple relationship. "You agreed to meet with me once a month to teach me about success," he persisted, prodding the memory of the ancient philosopher.

"Yes, yes," the master answered, also a bit annoyed. The presumption of this young man was infuriating. "I didn't expect you here so promptly," he added, lacing the final word with a note of censure.

"But you told me to be here by midmorning," Nikos protested.

"It's midmorning now."

Mediocrates looked directly into the young man's eyes. Without uttering a word, the old man issued a warning. Through his look alone, he disclosed impatience with Nikos as well as an unwillingness to allow a mere disciple to cast doubt on his authority.

"Are you here to learn, or to teach?" the philosopher finally queried, clearly rebuking his student.

A sheepish, almost whispered, response came from the young man's lips. "To learn, sir." Youthful eyes could no longer endure the glare of their aged counterparts, but cast their glance to the ground in submission.

"Let's begin, then," Mediocrates declared, confident in reasserted authority. "Come over to the steps."

Nikos walked toward the old philosopher, reconsidering everything that brought him here today. He had refused to acknowledge Penelope's contention that success is not about material gain or great accomplishments. He did not want to believe her words, yet somehow they never left his mind. However, in spite of her oft-offered encouragement to climb to the top of the mountain, Nikos had stubbornly insisted on learning from Mediocrates.

"What do you see here?" The query snapped the young man back to the present. The old man slowly swept his arm, palm up, toward the steps on which he sat.

"Steps carved into the hillside." Perplexed by his teacher's simple question, Nikos searched the old man's face for a clue.

"How do they compare to the Magistrate's Steps?"

Nikos considered the coarsely hewn steps more closely. The defects were obvious, even without careful examination. The Magistrate's Steps in Pouthena, on the other hand, were a source of pride for townsfolk. They sat flawless in front of the Square, an ideal introduction to the heart of town. How could he contrast the two without offending his master?

"Well, how do they compare?" Mediocrates insisted.

"Your steps, uh, suit the mountain," Nikos said hopefully, if not entirely truthfully. "The Magistrate's Steps suit Pouthena Square."

"Quite tactful, but not what I'm after. How do they compare?" the old man demanded, his tone echoing the tenacity of the question itself.

Nikos took a breath, then capitulated. "Your steps are inferior."

"How?" Mediocrates required, giving his pupil no time to regroup.

Seeing he had no choice but to answer, Nikos shifted from tact to vicious honesty. "The Magistrate's Steps are wide and level and magnificent. Yours are narrow, uneven, rough, and as ugly as any I've seen."

Smiling sadistically, the rumpled philosopher took an unexpected turn in his follow-up question. "But do they work?" he inquired.

Surprised and puzzled, the young man stood silent for a moment, trying to discern the master's intent. Unable to determine the reason, Nikos simply nodded.

"Exactly," a triumphant Mediocrates exclaimed. "And how long did it take for the Magistrate's Steps to be completed?"

Baffled by his teacher's bizarre and unrelenting interest in the Magistrate's Steps, Nikos answered to the best of his ability. "Almost half a year," he said, uncertain in tone and demeanor. Struggling to recall the history of his town, the disciple wondered what other outlandish questions the old philosopher might ask.

"And how many masons worked on your 'magnificent' steps?" Mediocrates sneered. His use of "your," combined with his emphasis on the word "magnificent," was an unmistakable reproach of Nikos for describing the Magistrate's Steps with such admiration.

"I'm not sure," he offered apologetically, "but I believe there were more than a dozen. Some came from towns and villages a week's journey from Pouthena," he added, unsure whether the old man would be pleased or upset at the additional information.

"Name them," he ordered.

Dumbfounded, Nikos searched his memory for any recollection of names. "I'm afraid I can't," he confessed. "The steps were built when I was a small boy."

"And that is my point," Mediocrates concluded, rising to his feet for the first time since Nikos had arrived. "That is my point."

The young man watched in disbelief as his master began to shuffle away. "I don't understand," he moaned plaintively. "None of this makes sense."

Turning toward his disciple, the old philosopher grinned with satisfaction. As usual, his explanation was uttered as a series of questions.

"Do the Magistrate's Steps perform any better than these?" he asked, waiting for Nikos to agree, which came with an uneasy shaking of the head. "And why would anyone work half a year to build steps that could be carved and set in place in a month?"

After pausing a moment to allow his protégé time to comprehend the significance of these questions, Mediocrates followed up with the final strike. "What's more, why would people work so hard for a town that will not remember them?"

Nikos began to understand. The steps here on the hillside were functional. They provided an adequate path from bottom to top and back again. True, they weren't attractive—in fact, they were an eyesore—but no one could deny that they fulfilled their purpose.

"Did you carve these yourself?" the young man asked in as humble a posture as he could manage. He certainly did not want his master to perceive the question as another challenge to his authority.

A slight smile crossed the face of the old philosopher, who had led his pupil to this question. "Yes, and before you ask, I did the job in a week."

Nikos studied the steps again. They had been carved directly into the granite of the hillside, so Mediocrates never had to locate and transport stone. The steps were crude, requiring little more than pick work to shape them.

"Life is hard enough," the teacher offered with a touch of empathy. "There's no sense in making it any harder on ourselves."

The young disciple considered these words of comfort. They appealed to him.

"Are you ready for the first rule of success?" the old man asked.

"Of course," he responded eagerly.

"First, do you remember the question I asked at the end of our last meeting?" Mediocrates inquired, putting on his sober-minded façade. Without waiting, he continued. "Are you willing to sacrifice all of your todays for a tomorrow that may never come?"

Nikos nodded in uncritical approval.

"Then never set unrealistic goals for yourself. This is your only life, so always consider your own comfort, and never demand too much of yourself."

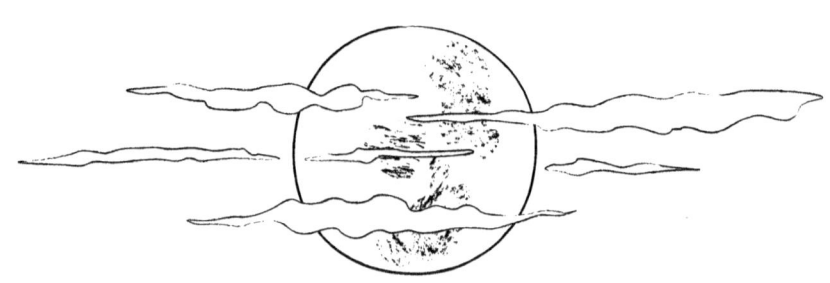

CHAPTER 4

IN THE
MOONLIGHT

S lipping from shadow to shadow, Nikos made his way down one of Pouthena's narrow streets. The town's white-washed homes, now painted cobalt blue by an impassive moon, seemed other-worldly to the young man who had known no other home.

The night's air was crisp, cold, and dry as Nikos inched stealthily toward the Square. Nothing else moved—nothing else should have moved. The fishermen, always the first to rise, would be stirring, but nowhere near the city center. Still, after the reception he had received the first time he returned from the mountain, the young disciple of Mediocrates wanted no one to know his actions, and especially not his thoughts.

Ever since Nikos had returned from his second encounter with the old philosopher, he had mulled over the differences between the unsightly granite steps built in a single week and the alabaster stairs at the entrance to the magistrate's court. The first were repulsive, though undeniably functional. The latter were also functional, but function somehow seemed secondary.

Turning the corner into the broad avenue that ended at the

Square, Nikos stopped short. The alabaster mesmerized the young man. For a moment Nikos forgot where he was and why. He simply stood, astounded by the silent beauty. In all his years growing up in Pouthena, the young man had never seen the steps in such splendor.

He had frequently seen the almost blinding white of the Magistrate's Steps at midday, and he had often felt the excitement of the steps at sunset, when they seemed to dance in a fiery orange-and-red exhibition. On a few occasions, he had even seen the steps greeting the sunrise in a celebration of pink and blue. But never had he seen them in this majestic deep blue.

"What brings you out so early, young man?"

Whirling to his left at this unexpected greeting, Nikos was stunned to see Demos standing just a few paces away. The town magistrate stood waiting for a response. His words were spoken gently, yet firmly, as though he had worn his authority so long that he now knew no other way.

The man's bearing was not in the least threatening, yet easily intimidated the less resolute among Pouthena's citizenry. In contrast, the young man before him stood uneasy and unsure. He shifted his weight from left to right, then back again, as he contemplated how to answer. Of all people to encounter at this hour, why did it have to be the magistrate?

"You're Nikos, aren't you?"

"Yes, my lord" were the only words the fearful young man could manage, and even these skulked out, ashamed to be spoken.

"Are you on an errand for Penelope?" the magistrate inquired, revealing a familiarity that surprised Nikos.

"No sir," the young man answered, this time with more vigor. As unwilling as he had been to share his plans and thoughts with anyone, Nikos was less willing to bring dishonor to Penelope. "I came here to think," he confided.

"That's why I'm here, too!" the older man asserted in a frank expression of camaraderie, a broad smile momentarily supplanting the gravity etched into his countenance. "I find the steps at this early hour ideal for contemplation."

Something about the manner of the stalwart judge in this shared moment was reassuring to Nikos. Perhaps it was the same thing that could make a father a source of comfort even while he maintained familial authority. The young man relaxed a little.

"I wanted to take a closer look at the steps," he offered. "I wanted to see them without the distractions of the day." Nikos stopped short of full disclosure, choosing not to mention a desire to keep secret his discipleship under Mediocrates.

Demos studied the face and bearing of the young man with eyes long accustomed to probing the hearts of citizens brought to his court. Nikos failed to notice, but this grandfatherly magistrate recognized the young man's reluctance to reveal his whole intent.

"What's so important about these steps?" The older man's question echoed the thoughts that had afflicted Nikos since his last encounter with Mediocrates.

"I don't know," the young man confessed, his voice divulging the turmoil within his heart. "They're beautiful...but what's the point?"

"Of beauty?" Demos asked, looking intently into the young man's eyes. "Tell me, what do you believe beauty to be?"

The question disquieted the disciple of Mediocrates. He was totally unprepared to answer. Besides, how could he define something so elusive as beauty?

"Perhaps that is too subjective a question," Demos interposed, noting the young man's restiveness. "Would you like to know my thoughts?"

Relieved, Nikos nodded.

"Beauty is more than form and color and texture. It is more than function, though often its companion. It can be created, but never engineered." Demos paused to allow his young companion a moment to absorb the discourse.

"What do you see when you look at these steps?"

"I see a way to reach your court, sir," Nikos said, unsure of the reason for the magistrate's question.

"Is that all you see?" he asked, placing decidedly more emphasis on the word "all." He clearly expected more of this young man.

Only minutes before Nikos had stood enraptured by the vision of the alabaster steps veiled in moonlight. Only minutes before he had sensed more than a mere pathway to the court, though he could not fully grasp what it was he was seeing. The sight of the steps had stopped him in his tracks. Now, though, he searched for an answer.

"The steps are beautiful," he answered, almost as a whisper. "But I don't understand why."

Demos smiled. "That's because beauty is more than the physical realm it inhabits. Beauty is not easy to define, yet impossible to ignore."

"But why should a dozen masons work half a year to build these steps, even if they are beautiful?" Nikos asked in frustration. "Why should any group go to so much trouble when a handful of masons could have built respectable steps in a month or two?"

"Because *respectable* steps can never do what these steps do," Demos replied, stressing *respectable* in rebuttal to the word's implicit claim. "*Respectable* steps can lift only your body. These steps lift your soul!"

Nikos glanced toward the steps again. Already the first hint of daylight was transforming the mesmerizing blues to a rose-tinted celebration of the new day. Nikos and Demos stood, side-by-side in silence, unwilling to spoil the moment with any more words.

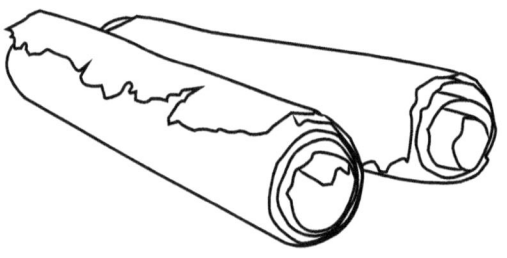

CHAPTER 5

TWO SCROLLS

Enshrouded in mist, the mountain resisted the trespasser struggling up its side. Nikos stopped to take his bearings, but could see nothing beyond the grey-white walls of fog. It was as though he had been locked into a lifeless, pale world.

Although the temperature was pleasant, the moisture in the air had now permeated his robe, forcing him to endure an unceasing chill. On top of that, movement was now uncomfortable as the robe clung to him, ruthlessly etching its path into each point of contact with his body. Even so, Nikos resumed his climb, painstakingly watching each of his own footsteps.

Twice before he had lost focus, and twice he had stumbled. The second time he had almost stepped off the trail and over the edge of a ravine. That misstep shook him, but Nikos had pushed forward, fighting to concentrate on the path before him, and striving to remember what he had seen during his previous trips up the mountain. This trip had taken much longer than those.

"Rough day for a hike, isn't it?"

Nikos stopped again, looking up to see the source of the

question. At first, he saw no one. The seemingly disembodied voice in this ethereal setting unnerved the young man, who flinched as soon as he saw movement in the corner of his eye. Swinging around to his left, Nikos caught sight of Mediocrates emerging from the veil of fog.

"You're a bit jumpy today," the old teacher said flatly.

"It's been a difficult climb," Nikos explained. "I almost fell into a ravine an hour ago."

"Is that so?" The words conveyed no alarm, nor was there any hint of sympathy. Instead, they belied the philosopher's lack of interest in his pupil. "I'm surprised you made the climb today."

Once again Nikos was disheartened by his mentor's dismissive attitude. He examined the old man standing before him. Wet, white hair lay matted against Mediocrates' scalp, a few strands having ventured onto his wrinkled forehead. The philosopher's pleated robe, drenched by the fog, hung heavily, revealing the outline of an unimpressive chest and shoulders.

"I'm here to learn from you," the young man said without much conviction. He had struggled up the mountain, committed to his purpose. Much of his enthusiasm, however, evaporated at the indifferent greeting of his teacher.

"I see," the old man said flatly. These words, too, were spoken without any real passion. "Well, I guess you'd better come with me, then." Turning abruptly, Mediocrates hiked back the same way he had come. Nikos quickly followed suit, fearing that he might lose the old man in the wall of white and grey that had so blighted his morning climb.

The occasional grunt, interspersed with the wheezing of his teacher, guided the disappointed disciple as they gradually wound their way along a narrow track. Suddenly, the old man stopped, just as the form of a hut rose up in front of master and student. It was the home of Mediocrates.

Nikos looked around with interest. Unlike the whitewashed masonry homes of Pouthena, this small structure was built of rough-hewn logs. An unsightly blend of twigs, leaves, and mud had been used to chink up the places where the logs did not fit together well. The tiny home also seemed to tilt to the left, though Nikos thought that impression might be caused by the slope of the building site.

"Wipe your sandals!" With these words, the teacher abruptly welcomed the pupil into his home.

The young man stepped through the threshold into a surprisingly warm room. The furnishings were sparse and crude, crafted merely to perform their intended functions. Nothing about them enticed the eye. Nothing about them lifted the soul. What did interest Nikos, however, was in the far corner—a pile of scrolls, unceremoniously heaped together.

"Have you read all those?" he asked, impressed by the collection. Never before had he seen so many in a private collection, and never before had he seen scrolls treated with such contempt. Most citizens of Pouthena owned no scrolls, though most had learned to read at the Academy. Literacy was a matter of pride for their community, and a scroll was always regarded as a treasure.

"What do you imagine I would learn from such a heap?" Mediocrates demanded with a glare. Clearly, he found the question insulting.

Once again stunned by his mentor's words, Nikos stood dumbfounded.

"Well, I asked a question. Will I be hearing an answer anytime soon?" the old man barked.

"Just about anything," the mystified young man replied

tentatively. Unsure what to do next, he stood still, watching the face of his master for some clue to an appropriate course of action.

"Perhaps you could enumerate the specific items that would be most enlightening," the sour old man stipulated, stressing the final word of the sentence with a cruel twist in his tone. "I would be delighted to learn from your extensive knowledge."

Nikos had made his trek up the mountain three times, and each time he had been surprised by the attitude and character of Mediocrates. Now, confronted by this bitter old philosopher over an innocent question, the young man wondered whether his efforts had been a waste of time. It could be that Stefanos was right in condemning the old man as "nothing but a faker."

Noticing the change in his pupil, Mediocrates changed his disposition.

"My dear Nikos!" the teacher exclaimed with an astounding new warmth in his voice. "I hope my technique has not alarmed you. My job is to push you to consider the world from a fresh perspective. That was the purpose of my questions." He uttered the last sentence plaintively, as though the young man's demeanor was an injustice to him personally.

"You seemed angry," was all the mystified young man could manage.

"Of course I did. Anger begets anger—and anger is one of the best tools for motivating a student." Smug silence followed this brief assertion, stated as an obvious truth. The old philosopher stood still, quite certain this claim had justified his behavior.

Not really satisfied with this justification, Nikos also stood still. Though looking into the face of his mentor, the young man found his thoughts drifting toward a new fear that easily overshadowed doubts about Mediocrates. Quitting now would mean admitting to Penelope that she had been right about the old man. Nikos wasn't ready to admit he was wrong.

"I see you're lost in thought," the now congenial teacher noted. "Yet time is precious, so let's begin today's lesson."

Nikos nodded, accepting the situation.

"Since you've demonstrated an interest in those scrolls, we'll begin with them. What do you imagine I would learn from such a heap?" Though the words of the question were the same ones he had used before, the tone was markedly different.

The young man's initial impulse was to answer naturally, as he had when Mediocrates first posed the question, but Nikos stopped himself, remembering the old philosopher's retort to his first answer. Feeling a bit defiant, Nikos chose a different response.

"I don't know for certain, but possibly one of those scrolls could teach us about manners."

The jab registered in the old man's eyes, but he demonstrated far more restraint than his pupil expected, even smiling at the irony.

"It just so happens that two of those scrolls address manners and customs. Let's take a look."

Mediocrates shuffled to the corner, reaching into the pile. Bent over with one arm immersed up to the elbow in the stack and the other braced against the wall, the old man rummaged around a bit. The image he presented, at variance with the presumed dignity of his station in life, prompted Nikos to chuckle. The young man could not see, but a dark grin crossed the lips of his mentor.

After a surprisingly short quest for the two manuscripts, Mediocrates extricated himself from his unflattering position, holding two scrolls up as proof of his triumph. He handed one to his student. "Read from the point where the edge is torn."

Nikos accepted the scroll, quickly finding the tear on the edge. "When you share the table with your better," he began, "defer to his rank. Take not until he takes, and take little when you do."

"Do you understand?" The philosopher's manner and tone were disarming, driving away the doubt Nikos had felt only minutes before. "What's more, do you agree?"

The young man thought for a moment, then nodded. Penelope had always taught him to respect everyone, but to defer to anyone of rank or position. She was not encouraging her adopted son to be a sycophant, but she was a realist nonetheless. She always maintained a clear distinction between the demands of etiquette and those of conscience. Deference in the first was a small price to pay for peace; deference in the latter was unthinkable.

"I'd like you to read from this one now," Mediocrates asked, handing the second scroll to his protégé. "You can begin where my thumb is."

Nikos exchanged scrolls with the old man, carefully noting where he should start reading. "A citizen's highest vocation is hospitality, especially to those in greatest need." The young man looked up expectantly, wondering what lesson the bedraggled philosopher would draw from these readings.

"Please continue," he requested.

"A virtuous host always defers to his guest, no matter how common or poor." Nikos's words trailed off a bit as he finished the sentence, recognizing the discrepancy Mediocrates had brought to light.

"Once again, do you understand? And do you agree?" the old man asked, this time with a slightly sharper tone.

Nikos reconsidered the two statements. On the surface, both seemed right, but taken together, they clearly contradicted one another. He stood in the hut of his mentor, unable to answer.

"Tell me," Mediocrates continued, "what have you learned? How have these scrolls profited you?" The old man had again donned a brusque and authoritative air.

"They haven't taught me anything I did not already know," Nikos offered, more out of obligation than conviction.

"Exactly!" That single word, uttered so confidently and purposefully by the teacher, conveyed much to the student. First, it was clear that Mediocrates had anticipated the course of the conversation from the start. But the word also impressed on Nikos that he had never really studied with a critical eye.

Mediocrates observed the signs of agitation written on the face of his young student, whose brow was furrowed and lips turned down. Now was the time to drive home the lesson.

"At the risk of alarming you again," the old man said with a trace of sarcasm, "I'll repeat my earlier question." Then, gesturing toward the pile of scrolls, he asked, "What do you imagine I would learn from such a heap?"

Nikos glanced once again at the scrolls. He understood the gist of his mentor's teaching, but could not bring himself to say it. Instead, he turned toward Mediocrates and waited to be told.

The old man sensed that his pupil was ready for his next truth. "The world is filled with scrolls. Some are better than others, but they are all the product of human imagination. And just as people have trouble getting along, scrolls argue and contradict and lie."

Mediocrates paused a moment to gauge the effect of his discourse on the bewildered young man before him. "The point is, no scroll is better than a person. And no person has seen and done what you have. So don't bother with the advice of fools! Live life your way!"

CHAPTER 6

KEEPER OF THE SCROLLS

A week had passed since his last trip up the mountain, yet all week Nikos had found it difficult to focus on his work. Today, as he traversed the streets delivering packages for Penelope, he still fought to remain focused. Finally, he found himself making his last delivery for the day.

"Thanks again, and be sure to give our love to Penelope!" The old woman smiled with genuine warmth, watching as Nikos turned to go. Her eyes followed the preoccupied young man as he first headed down the path from her door, but then she, too, turned. When she went inside, the young man heard the click of the door latch, though he was already a dozen paces away.

Nikos grinned. There were still several hours before sunset, so today he could finally visit the Academy. Funny, he thought. Just a year before, when he was a pupil—especially when he was close to finishing his studies—every thought seemed to revolve around the adventure life would hold when he would no longer be a student. When he was at the Academy, he could think only of leaving!

How things had changed! Ever since his last trip up the

mountain—during the week Nikos had been back in Pouthena—his every thought seemed fixed on the Academy. More specifically, he could not stop thinking about the collection of scrolls in the reading chamber. Pouthena's citizens were proud of their Academy, and they were proud of its collection of scrolls.

No one, of course, was prouder than Sophia, who had long been entrusted with the collection. Sophia had been there as long as Nikos could remember, guarding each precious scroll as though it were a treasure. In fact, she seemed to know each one intimately. She knew the creases, the rips, the smudges, and the flaws, but she also knew the character and personality of each. For Sophia, who had dedicated herself to education, those scrolls were truly her children, and she would allow no one to hurt them.

What a contrast with Mediocrates! Although he had amassed a sizeable collection of scrolls himself, he viewed them with disdain. What's more, he treated them much as he would stray dogs. As Nikos recalled the pile of scrolls strewn across the floor of his mentor's home, he imagined the horror that Sophia would experience if she were to see them.

He had waited a week for the opportunity to speak with her, but as he drew closer to the Academy, his patience seemed to disappear altogether. At last the road curved around Daskalos Hill and the Academy came into view. The young man unconsciously quickened his pace as legs and feet raced to keep up with thought and feeling.

When he finally reached the steps in front of the portico, Nikos paused a moment, relishing memories and reflections and images of countless days he had spent here. Like many young men, he had denied his own feelings of joy in this place of learning, especially in the presence of his peers. Now, though, as he stood here alone, he could no longer deny those feelings.

"Nikos? Is that you?" a tentative voice asked. The returned pupil spun around just in time to see Sophia hurrying toward him.

"Why, it is!" she cried out, this time without any note of reserve in her voice. There was a real sense of delight in her words. "What brings you back to the Academy, young man?"

"I came to see you," Nikos pronounced with a deliberate satisfaction. "I've been thinking about the scrolls," he said more somberly. "I've got some questions."

"What kind of questions?" Sophia asked, this time with the same searching expression she often wore when students came to her in the Academy's reading chamber. "How can I help you?" she continued, puzzled by this unusual meeting.

"Would it be possible to speak in the chamber?" Nikos said, a bit defensively. His manner seemed out-of-place to his elderly confidant, who remembered the young man as open, friendly, and honest, though sometimes a bit brash as a student. She could never remember a time when he had been so secretive.

"Alright. We'll go there now," she acquiesced, "if that suits you." Nikos simply nodded, prompting her to turn back up the steps. When she reached the western end of the portico, she unlocked the main door into the reading chamber.

Almost immediately a flood of memories assailed the former student. At times this room had seemed like a prison, separating him from the wonders of the world outside. More often, though, the room had been the port of departure for his journeys of discovery. From this room he had explored the seas, walked the streets of big cities, and witnessed wars. In this room he had discovered the magic of math and uncovered the secrets of people long dead.

"What did you want to ask me?" Sophia asked with gentleness.

Her face revealed the growing concern in her heart.

Taking a deep breath first, Nikos opened up. "I've been up the mountain," he confided. "I've become a student of a philosopher I met there."

"Have you met Hypatos, then?" the elderly woman gasped, her face animated with excitement.

"No, that's not his name," the young man stated flatly. "I'm studying with Mediocrates."

Excitement disappeared, and concern once again took up residence on Sophia's face. Mixed with the concern was a trace of disapproval that did not go unnoticed.

After his experience with Penelope, Nikos had anticipated the possibility of a similar reaction from Sophia. He had decided he would confide in her, regardless of her reaction. Even so, the judgment in her features disappointed him.

"Mediocrates has a sizeable collection of scrolls," the young man began.

"Yes, I know!" Sophia interrupted, her retort laced with an unmistakable scorn.

"You've seen his scrolls?" Nikos asked, astonished by the revelation. "When?"

"That's not important now. I really don't care to discuss him or his crude habits," she said, dismissing Mediocrates with a passion in her voice that surprised Nikos. "I will try to answer your questions, though."

The young man shifted uneasily, carefully studying the face of his one-time mentor and friend. She had always been there for him, and she had always helped him see things more clearly. He had had difficult conversations with her before, speaking not only about the scrolls, but about the problems of adolescence. He trusted her then, and he trusted her now.

"Mediocrates opened my eyes to something," Nikos confided. "He compared scrolls to people, explaining that just as people often do not get along with each other, scrolls contradict one another. He even said that scrolls lie." As he uttered the last statement, the young man looked intently at Sophia for confirmation.

Sighing a little before speaking, she collected her thoughts. "It's true. Scrolls do contradict one another. And some scrolls lie."

Nikos's heart sank. As long as he could remember, he had regarded scrolls as a treasure of knowledge and understanding. Now, though, Sophia's words confirmed his worst fears. It was as though a rock had been overturned, revealing foul little creatures wriggling and scurrying and scampering away. How could he ever trust a scroll again? And why should he bother?

Sophia read his face, recognizing in it the inevitable disillusionment of youthful idealism. "You know, I believe, that I place great value in scrolls," she began, choosing her words cautiously. Her tone was firm, yet warm. "Each one is a friend, to be cherished just as you would one of your companions."

Pausing a moment, Sophia looked directly into Nikos's eyes. "Has Stefanos ever told you something incorrect?" she asked suddenly.

"You mean lied?" Nikos asked, surprised by the question.

"Whether by intent or in error does not matter at the moment," Sophia stated bluntly. "I simply want to know whether he has ever told you something that you already knew to be wrong or later discovered to be false."

"Yes, of course." The words, offered hesitantly, reflected Nikos's confusion over the course of the conversation. He searched Sophia's face in hopes of detecting her objective.

"Is he still your friend?"

Spoken with the gentleness characteristic of Sophia's speech and behavior, the sentence was nevertheless unusual in its intensity. She wasn't merely asking a question. Through her tone, she was requiring Nikos to consider carefully before answering.

"Yes." The single word emerged stiffly from bewildered lips. He stood captive before this aged, wispy, white-haired woman half his size.

"Why?" was her simple response.

Again Nikos was surprised. "I cannot remember a time when we weren't friends," he said, more as a reflection of his thoughts than an answer to her question. "Besides, everyone makes mistakes," he added, this time with greater confidence.

"And that's the way it is with scrolls!"

"But what's the point?" Nikos exclaimed. "Why should I bother studying scrolls if I can't trust them?" he added in frustration.

"Do you believe Stefanos now?" Sophia asked. The slender keeper-of-the-scrolls wore that impish look on her face Nikos had seen so many times before. He knew an answer to his questions was close.

"Yes, of course," he replied plaintively. "He's one of my closest friends!"

"That's precisely the way we must view our parchment and papyrus companions. Just as the scribes who wrote them make mistakes, so, too, do our scrolls."

"But I know Stefanos," Nikos objected. "I know his character, and I know I can trust him. He would never lie to me. I don't know any of the people who wrote these scrolls, though. Why should I trust them?"

"Because you must," Sophia insisted. "Because you must."

Moments before Nikos had been sure Sophia was close to providing him a satisfactory answer. Now it seemed she had headed off in another direction altogether.

"Why?" His question was an expression of frustration rather than one of defiance.

"Without scrolls, our world is petty and brutish. Without scrolls our world is void of ideas and beauty and hope." Sophia paused briefly, considering Nikos's reaction. "Without scrolls, life can be no bigger than what we can see and hear and smell and touch and taste ourselves."

"How can I know what is true?" Nikos pleaded. He wanted a reason to trust again.

"How do you know what is true when you converse with a friend?" Sophia answered. "How do you know when Stefanos is right or when he is wrong?"

"Because I know Stefanos!" came the exasperated response. "I know his character. I know his heart. I grew up with him, so I know as much about him as anyone. He isn't wrong often, and he never lies!"

"Would it be fair for a stranger to judge him?" Sophia asked.

"Of course not," Nikos said quietly, beginning to understand his old friend's logic.

"That's the way it is with scrolls. Only after we come to know them can we truly judge them," Sophia said. "That's not to say that all scrolls are worth our friendship. But we become better judges of scrolls—and people—the more we interact with them."

The young man stood before the diminutive keeper-of-the-scrolls without saying a word. Reflecting on the time he had spent in the reading chamber, he saw the truth in Sophia's words. It seemed odd to him now that he had never recognized this truth. He had always had favorites among the scrolls, and he had always found some to be less useful. Somehow, he had never stopped to evaluate their relative merit.

"There's something else," Sophia interjected, seeing in Nikos's silence a growing awareness. "Understanding is more than mere accumulation of information. You can memorize the words of any scroll, but doing so does not mean you will understand. To understand, you must judge. And to judge the value of any one scroll, you must know many other scrolls."

"How do I know which scrolls to use?" the young man asked.

"Any and all!" Sophia cried out excitedly. "The more you interact with your friends, the more you understand the world around you."

Listening earnestly, Nikos smiled at the word "friends." He remembered the many times he had heard Sophia refer to scrolls as though they were people. Some of the boys had made fun of her, but all of them knew the elderly woman deeply loved the scrolls in her care.

The smile dissipated as he called to mind his last meeting with Mediocrates. "What about scrolls that contradict one another, or worse, scrolls that lie?" Nikos asked more somberly.

"You've asked two questions, young man," Sophia replied. "Let's address the case of contradictions first. You tell me the contradiction that brought you here."

Straightening up a bit, Nikos struggled to remember the wording of the two scrolls from which he had read during his discussion with Mediocrates. "I don't remember the precise wording," the young man admitted, "but one scroll advocated always deferring to your better when dining. The other scroll claimed that the highest duty of a citizen is hospitality, especially to people in need."

"How do these scrolls contradict?"

Nikos did not expect the question. To him, the contradiction was obvious.

"The first scroll insists that a person defer to his better," he explained. "The second suggests that the more noble individual must defer to all guests, even the lesser ones who are common or poor."

"I won't bother addressing your assumption that a poor person is necessarily lesser than someone who isn't," Sophia stated with an air of authority. "What I will ask you to consider is context. What is the context of the first statement?"

"I don't know," Nikos said defensively. "I read only what Mediocrates asked me to read."

"And that is your biggest mistake," the diminutive yet enthusiastic woman declared. "Without context, you cannot understand anything! I'm not familiar with those scrolls, but this much I can tell you. The first is addressed to the person you consider the lesser. The second is addressed to the individual you consider the better. That understanding alone is enough to dismiss any idea of contradiction in this case."

"How?" Nikos objected.

"It would seem that in neither case is the scribe attempting to state universal truth. Rather, each scribe is offering advice to individuals in specific circumstances," Sophia explained. "When you think you perceive a contradiction among scrolls, consider context. Then consider the intended audience. If you still have a contradiction, consider the culture of the scribe and the year when the scroll was written. When you do, many of your supposed contradictions will disappear."

"What about those that don't?" Nikos asked, desperately seeking some avenue of intellectual vindication.

"That's when you use your head, young man!" Sophia looked

intently at her young friend, then walked over to a rack. Running her finger along a row of scrolls stored neatly on the rack, she selected one, turning back toward Nikos. "Read this passage from Hesiod," she directed.

Nikos took the scroll from her, careful to treat it with the same respect the elderly woman expected. "But he who neither thinks for himself nor learns from others, is a failure as a man."

"Scrolls are not a replacement for thinking," Sophia declared. "To gain the most from them, you must use your head. But without scrolls, you'll never go as far, see as much, or live as well. And by the way.... I recommend you set aside some time to read more of this scroll for context!"

Rather sheepishly, Nikos asked his last question. "What about scrolls that lie?"

Sighing first, Sophia answered. "Unfortunately, some of our acquaintances are liars. Not many, but some. Even these, though, can help you understand."

"How?"

"Any scroll that makes you think is a scroll that helps you," the old woman said, smiling at her young friend. "Even liars among our scrolls can teach us...if we use our heads!"

CHAPTER 7

WAITING FOR THE RIGHT MOMENT

Nikos was beginning to regret his decision to climb the mountain today. When he set out, the morning was already cold. The sky above the mountain and in front of him had been blue and cloudless, but dark clouds in the seaward sky behind him had imbued them with hate. Even so, he had left, determined to meet Mediocrates for his monthly lesson.

The clouds had pushed toward the mountain as though intent on beating Nikos to his destination. The mood of the mountain and the sky above it grew more hostile with each step the young man took. Freezing rain had begun falling sporadically an hour before, but now the sky was angrily spitting its hatred, transforming the mountain trail into a muddy rivulet. The mountain itself seemed to hiss and murmur as slushy ice trickled through barren tree branches and oozed across patches of lifeless brown grass and brush.

Stopping a moment to gauge his progress, Nikos looked around for a familiar landmark. Nothing! The forests had become legions of brown skeletons, reaching upward with thousands of gnarled and twisted fingers to an unsympathetic sky. Chamelion-like grass and shrubs had abandoned their more lively green hues for the dismal brown shades of mountain soil. Half frozen torrents had etched new features into the trail itself, making it unrecognizable. Everything was different!

Judging his progress almost entirely on time spent climbing, Nikos once again pushed on, believing he had to be close to the home of his mentor. Quickly reestablishing his pace, the young man trudged on, each step protested by the slurping and sucking of disgruntled mud and ice clinging to his boots.

Finally he saw a feature he recognized. Roughly a hundred yards ahead lay the rock wall he had seen during his first climb. Nikos stopped once more. It was at this point that he had first set eyes on Mediocrates. Cold and wet, the young man turned toward the stump where the aged philosopher had been perched that day. It was ridiculous, of course, to imagine the old man waiting there in this weather, but Nikos looked anyway. Just a stump!

Studying the area to get his bearings, the young disciple recognized the granite steps where he had seen his teacher the second time. During his last trip up the mountain, he had climbed those steps in the fog to follow a path leading to the home of Mediocrates. Even though the old man had explicitly told him not to visit his home uninvited, Nikos decided abruptly that he would go there again. Slogging across an icy patch of dead grass, he turned onto the path.

A dense cover of branches hung over the little path. Although these trees were as barren as the trees Nikos had seen all along the mountain trail, the branches were thick. They were also draped in a mass of tangled, lifeless vines. The stark, naked canopy partially shielded the path from the worst of the ice, leaving it muddy, but far easier to traverse.

From time to time Nikos stopped to take a good look at his surroundings. During his previous experience on the path, fog had concealed virtually everything. Now the areas on either side of the path were clear, though bleak in appearance.

As the path wound around a particularly thick cluster of trees and into a small meadow bordered by a shallow ravine, a peculiar structure came into view. The rough-hewn log building had a roof, one complete wall, and three other walls in various stages of completion. Obvious signs of weathering made it clear that at least a decade had passed since work had been done on this unusual edifice. Nikos concluded that whoever had started this structure had abandoned it.

For most of this morning's journey, the exertion of plodding through mud had kept the disciple of Mediocrates warm. Now, though, he felt a growing chill. It was time to move on.

Nikos quickened his pace, partly to warm up, but partly to cut short the time to his mentor's home. He had agreed to mid-morning meetings with Mediocrates, but noon was approaching. Fortunately, the tiny log hut wasn't far, and Nikos found himself at the door in minutes.

Just as the young man lifted his knuckles toward the door, it opened.

"What are you doing here?" Mediocrates barked, the sour look on his face matching the biting tone of his voice. "I directed you never to come uninvited!"

Nikos had expected this sort of reception, not only because he had ignored a rule the old man established during their last session, but because he had come to understand his mentor's demeanor. Mediocrates was rarely pleasant and easily aggravated. He was often disrespectful and even rude. At first

Nikos had found him quite intimidating, but the young disciple had grown accustomed to his grumpy mentor.

"I came for my lesson," Nikos said with restraint, but with a newfound confidence as well. "You weren't where I expected you to be," he added sharply, "so I came here."

Mediocrates stood in the doorway, grimly examining his pupil. Recognizing a change in Nikos, he curbed his own impulse to lash out at the young man's impudent disregard for propriety. The old philosopher chose to set aside his anger for the moment. Putting on a mask of hospitality, he invited Nikos inside.

"Well don't stand there in this nasty weather, young man! Come inside." With a sweep of his right arm and a disingenuous smile, Mediocrates ushered the errant pupil into his home.

Nikos stepped inside, grateful to be somewhere dry and warm.

"Perhaps you'd like to remove your boots?" the white-haired philosopher asked in as pleasant a voice as he could manage. "And there's a hook for your cloak," he noted, pointing to a coarse peg. The hook protruded from a slot between two logs in the wall. It was one of four, each at a different angle to the wall and each of a different size. Uneven spacing among the four hooks accentuated the sense of disorder.

"I saw an odd building on the way here," Nikos declared. "It's unfinished, and it looks as though no one has worked on it for years."

"Is that so," the old man said coolly. Intending to ignore the statement, Mediocrates stood in impassive silence, a disapproving scowl issuing a warning to his disciple.

"Do you know what it was supposed to be?" Nikos asked, fully aware that it was not a question his teacher cared to address.

"I do," the old man said. "But that's not a topic for today."

Perceiving a doggedness in his student, he offered a compromise. "Let's attend to that subject next time. For now, take a seat."

Nikos looked around, noticed a low chair with a couple of pillows on it, and then sat down. Mediocrates stepped over to a taller chair a couple of feet away and sat facing his disciple.

"What is today's lesson?" the young man asked, a bit impulsively.

"Wait a moment," the tired old teacher said. "Wait for the right moment."

The young man stared at Mediocrates expectantly, but the old man sat in silence, head down as though collecting his thoughts. Nikos kept silent himself, waiting for his teacher to begin. The white-haired philosopher remained silent and still. His slow, steady breathing marked the passing of time.

Several minutes passed. Nikos grew impatient, reluctantly choosing to wait quietly. As he did, his mentor's steady breathing gradually became louder, eventually revealing itself in a snort.

Nikos stood suddenly. "Is this what you call a lesson?" he roared, waking his teacher.

Mediocrates opened his eyes slowly. "Why, yes, I guess it is," he yawned. Then, with a roguish grin, he completed his thought: "Yes, I would call this your most important lesson to date!"

"All you've done is fall asleep while I've waited patiently," Nikos protested. "How does that teach me anything?"

"My falling asleep teaches you precisely what you need to know," the old man countered. "In fact, based on your behavior today, the lesson is particularly timely."

Nikos stared at his teacher blankly, trying to make sense of his words. Mediocrates simply sat, still wearing his insulting grin. Deciding to engage his instructor in this battle of wills, Nikos sat down again, defiantly crossing his arms and aggressively waiting for an explanation.

A few minutes passed. Finally, the old teacher stood up, clearing his throat as though to make a noteworthy statement.

"Very good, young man," Mediocrates declared. "Very good, indeed."

Nikos's arms dropped to his sides as the defiance in his eyes yielded to bewilderment.

Noting the change in his student's face, Mediocrates continued. "You've demonstrated an ability to wait just now. That is the crux of today's lesson."

"I don't understand," Nikos said slowly. "How is waiting a lesson?"

"Where did you find me today?" the old man asked.

"At your home, of course. But what does that have to do with anything?"

"Everything," Mediocrates exclaimed. "We generally meet for our lessons close to the trail, but not today. When I saw the storm approaching, I decided not to head outside. Anyone with any sense would have done likewise!"

"But we had an agreement!" Nikos objected.

"Yes, I'm quite well aware of that," the old man snarled. "But no meeting is important enough to risk life and limb to keep. I chose to stay home. You chose to act foolishly!"

Resenting his mentor's characterization of his morning trek, Nikos scowled.

"I'll ask you again," the white-haired philosopher continued. "Where did you find me today?"

"I've already told you," the young man answered in exasperation. "At home!"

"Precisely!" Mediocrates proclaimed with an air of victory. "I chose not to risk the elements. Did I miss anything?" Without waiting for an answer, the old man finished his line of thinking. "No, you came to me. That is the point!"

Nikos sat in confusion, unable to follow his teacher's logic. He asked no more questions. After a few moments of uncomfortable silence for his student, Mediocrates spoke up.

"I see you've learned your lesson, though you don't understand it," he said, delighted in the seeming absurdity of his words. "You're waiting for my explanation, and that is the point."

"What is the point?" Nikos pleaded.

"Whenever life presents obstacles that are too challenging, or conditions that are too threatening," Mediocrates explained smugly, "the best strategy is to wait—wait for the right moment. I chose not to venture outside today, but missed nothing. You came to me."

The young man sat still, struggling with the concept.

"Once you entered my home, we sat down," the old man continued. "I made you wait for your lesson while I slept. And that was the lesson. Remember, whatever your goal, don't push too hard for it. It'll eventually come to you if it's meant to be."

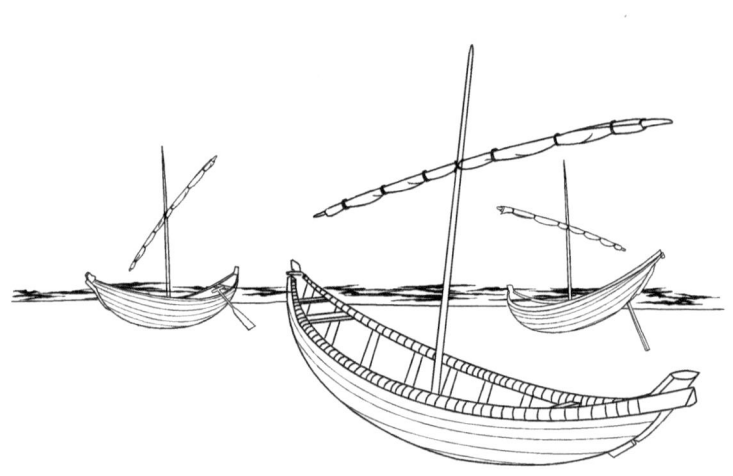

CHAPTER 8

NEVER STOP MOVING

Seating himself on a flat section of driftwood, Nikos marveled that such a colossal tree should end up on the beach near his home. The young man, who prided himself on his knowledge of the trees around Pouthena, did not recognize this wood. Countless days at sea had worn away much of the wood's natural character. Whatever the tree's species and whatever its former state, this evening it was as good a spot as any from which to watch the beach.

Ever since he was old enough to slip away from home, he had enjoyed coming to this spot at the edge of the town's small harbor. From his vantage point he could watch the fishermen returning from their day's work at sea, only to begin their work on shore. Each boat had to be secured. Nets and sails needed mending. And then there was the catch!

Women from the town would congregate on shore, chatting pleasantly with one another while waiting for that night's dinner to arrive. As the boats came in, though, the once convivial group quickly morphed into a clamoring horde intent on buying the best for their families. The contest, which somehow never marred their friendships, was a spectacle Nikos always enjoyed.

Tonight Nikos had missed the homecoming of most of the town's fleet, but he did not mind. He could still watch Andreas, whom he considered to be the most intriguing of Pouthena's fishermen. Coarse, short-cropped hair without any hint of color seemed at odds with the intense bronze of the old fisherman's sun-baked skin. His small, wiry frame belied the surprising strength in this man, who worked as hard as his sons, and even grandsons now learning the trade.

No one in town disputed their unique talent for bringing in the finest and largest sea bass and tuna, two of the most desired varieties. It was for that reason that the greatest commotion occurred when Andreas and his sons returned. On many days they returned last, and often only when deep crimson and purple streaks in the Western sky were yielding to the moon and stars.

As Nikos mused on previous evenings he had passed on the beach, three boats appeared at the harbor entrance, their naked masks silhouetted against a darkening sky. When the small flotilla approached, the rhythmic splashing of oars harmonized with the steady lapping of waves.

Andreas and his youngest son occupied the first boat to reach shore. The old sailor jumped from his seat into knee-high water in a single, fluid motion, grabbing a tow rope in the bow. His son jumped out a moment later, taking hold of the stern. The old man pulled, the young man pushed, and the boat slid onto wet sand. The second and third boats, crewed by his other sons and grandsons, were just moments behind. At the same time, the women who had waited for the best catch converged on the tiny fleet.

"Andreas! Andreas!" one woman yelled mournfully. "I've waited nearly an hour for one of your sea bass," she added, staking her claim based on seniority.

"Tuna for me!" a tiny woman shrieked, not feeling familiar enough with the old fisherman to call out his name. "I have four sons and three daughters to feed," she continued, pleading her case based on need.

Working quickly with his sons and grandsons, Andreas brought the day's catch up to the *Fishmonger's Pavillion*. The weathered wooden deck had been in place as long as Nikos could remember, yet he had never seen fishmongers there. Instead, the fishermen all used the rough structure to sell their catch directly to townsfolk.

From his vantage point on the driftwood, Nikos watched with both amusement and keen interest—amusement at the frantic spirit of the women rushing to buy the best fish, but keen interest in the unruffled disposition of Andreas. The day's catch had been plentiful, yet the veteran fisherman orchestrated an efficient series of transactions that left everyone happy.

Soon the women were all headed home to their families. Shortly after securing the three boats, the sons and grandsons of Andreas also headed home to their families. He was alone, seated at the pavillion with one of his sails. Nikos observed as the old sailor ran his hand up and down the fabric of the sail checking for small tears or weaknesses. Impulsively, the young man stood up and strode over to the object of his interest.

"Well hello, young man," Andreas called out. "If you've come for the catch, I'm afraid you're too late," he added apologetically.

"No, that's not why I'm here," Nikos answered. "Whenever I can, I enjoy watching the boats return. I've been watching from that log over there."

Andreas turned toward the large piece of driftwood, then turned back toward Nikos, smiling. "I guess we put on quite a show, don't we?"

"Yes," was all the young man said, partly because he was suddenly embarrassed at revealing his habit of spying on neighbors, but mainly because he wanted to speak with Andreas about more important issues. "Actually, I've got a question for you, if you don't mind," Nikos disclosed meekly.

The weathered but still vibrant face of the aged fisherman wore a look of surprise. "What kind of question do you have for an old salt like me?"

Nikos took a deep breath as though preparing to exert himself. "I'm interested in success," he explained. "You're the most successful fisherman in Pouthena. You have been—all my life. I came here to watch, as always, but when I saw you alone, I thought...." The young man did not finish his sentence, suddenly ashamed at intruding on Andreas.

"You thought I could give you some easy answers," the fisherman said, pausing a moment in reflection. "I'll be happy to answer your questions, though you may not find the answers to your liking," he continued. "And they most certainly won't be easy!"

Nikos stood before Andreas, delighted that the old sailor had agreed to speak with him, but not really sure where to begin. While the young man hesitated, the veteran fisherman studied his face.

"You're Nikos, aren't you?" he asked abruptly. "You've certainly grown!" he added, not giving the young man the opportunity to answer. "And how is Penelope these days?"

Being recognized shocked Nikos, but not as much as the fisherman's familiarity with Penelope. To the young man's knowledge, his adopted mother never came to the harbor and Andreas never ventured beyond the harbor. He even lived in a cottage within a stone's throw of the harbor beach.

"I haven't seen her much since the year of dying," the wiry old man continued, but now in a distinctively wistful tone. His unruffled bearing evaporated, even as he lowered his head and turned away from Nikos.

The young man stood still, feeling awkward and a bit ashamed.

"Should I go?" he asked, completely unprepared to face the old man's pain. Nikos always felt useless when confronted with grief or anguish, but especially when a situation pounced on him unexpectedly. He never knew what to say!

Andreas held up an arm in response, but kept his head turned. The flat palm of his hand, extended toward the young man, told him not to go, but also asked that he wait a moment.

Nikos did wait, his own head turned down. As he stood there, uneasily shifting his weight from time to time, he recalled moments when he had watched Penelope comforting friends. She rarely seemed at a loss for words, and somehow her words were always just right. He himself had experienced her gift many times, mostly after silly childhood tragedies. Unfortunately, he had no such knack for comforting people in pain.

"What, exactly, is your question?" The words, though spoken softly, intruded on Nikos's memories and brought him back to the beach. He looked up, this time to see an upturned face with no obvious sign of sorrow.

"As I said earlier, I'm interested in success," he replied. "What is it you do that makes you so successful?"

Andreas did not hesitate, even for an instant. "I push."

After a brief moment, Nikos realized the veteran fisherman had finished his thought.

"I don't understand. What do you push?"

"Myself!" Andreas exclaimed the single word with such enthusiasm that Nikos retreated a little. Almost immediately, the old fisherman jumped to his feet, wrapping an arm around his young friend.

"Let me show you something," he insisted, shoving his hand against Nikos's back. The unanticipated thrust gave him no choice but to walk forward.

"Do you understand now?" Andreas asked, a broad smile thoroughly displacing any lingering sadness.

"Not really," the young man answered, puzzled by this apparently irrelevant demonstration. "I understand that you pushed me, but what does that have to do with success?"

"Everything!" the wiry sailor yelped. "Success in anything takes work—hard work. And the greater the success, the more effort you need. Are you following me?"

"I think so," Nikos said cautiously, afraid to appear dim-witted.

Andreas saw through the pretense right away.

"Whatever you do in life, you'll encounter headwinds." The fisherman looked directly at the young man with an intensity that matched the passion in his speech. "And you'll always have plenty of excuses for stopping. But if you want to succeed, you can never stop!"

The last two words exploded out of his mouth, their meaning reverberating through Nikos's memories of his last encounter with Mediocrates.

"What if moving forward is dangerous?" the young man countered without real conviction.

"Never stop!" Andreas insisted. "There's always a way to move forward. You just have to find that way."

"Would you put out to sea in a tempest?" Nikos asked

defensively.

"Of course not!" the veteran sailor barked. "But I don't stop. I press forward."

The young man stood silent, struggling to comprehend the enigma put forth by the wiry, energetic old sailor facing him.

"If you don't put out to sea during a tempest," Nikos asked in frustration, "then how do you 'press forward.' I don't understand."

"I'll answer, but only after you answer my questions," Andreas challenged. "What things must a fisherman do to be successful?"

"Catch fish!"

A quick look of disapproval swept the smug look from Nikos's face.

"Anything else?" Andreas demanded.

"You have to throw your nets in the right spot," the young man answered. Then, remembering the words of Mediocrates, he added another thought: "And then you wait for the right moment."

Laughter issued from deep within the fisherman-teacher, whose whole body pulsated uncontrollably. Once again, Nikos stood speechless, this time waiting for the laughter to stop.

"Thanks, young man. That moment was exactly what I needed!" the old sailor said, genuinely grateful for the simple joy of the moment. "Do you really think fishing is that simple?"

"I guess not," Nikos said, looking down at his feet while wishing he'd never begun this conversation. "I guess there must be something you do that others don't. I don't know what, though."

Andreas smiled. "Yes, there's actually more than one 'something' I do. When a storm or tides prevent me from putting out to sea, I may patch up my boats, or mend my nets, or repair my sails. That way I'm ready when the tides and weather are right."

The young man listened intently, but said nothing.

Seeing the effect his words had already made on the young man before him, the passionate old sailor pressed his case. "The point is," he said, "I always push myself. If I don't, no one else will. And one thing I've learned is that you'll never get anywhere without moving forward!"

Nikos considered the words of his new friend, still silent.

"Oh, and 'waiting for the right moment,' as you put it, works only when you prepare," Andreas added. "Then, when the time is right, you'll be ready to push through to your goals."

CHAPTER 9

A BROKEN BLADE

Nikos stopped. The trail before him ended abruptly at a ravine that had not been there during his previous visits to the mountain. Loose rock and gravel lined the bottom of this chasm, testifying to the power of water frantically seeking a resting place. He could see where the trail picked up at the far side of this gorge, but immediately realized he could neither jump across nor climb down one side and back up the other.

The ravine ran the entire width of the shelf that lay between the rock mountainside 20 paces to his left and the drop-off 30 paces to his right. Nikos kicked a fist-sized rock in frustration, and then watched it hit the gorge halfway down its far side. As the rock worked its way to the bottom, it wheedled and cajoled other rocks and pebbles to join in its pilgrimage.

Movement subsided as quickly as it had begun, surrendering to silence. That silence taunted the young man, as though proclaiming that further movement would not be permitted. Irritated, he sat down to consider his options. The easiest choice would be quitting. He could simply turn around and head back down the mountain. Nikos quickly dismissed the idea—he was not ready to quit!

A second option would be to explore the area, looking for another trail. Even as he considered the thought, and even though a different route would solve his dilemma, Nikos knew in his heart that it likely did not exist. No one had ever suggested such a possibility to him. Besides, the contour of the mountain made another trail unlikely.

"So where does that leave me?" he thought out loud. "I won't go home, and I can't go forward!"

He stood up again, impatient to be on his way. Without consciously deciding to pace the length of the ravine's rim, Nikos found himself doing just that. As he walked, first up toward the rock mountainside to the left of the trail, then down toward the drop-off to the right, he realized that his only remaining option was to bridge the gorge. But how? He had no tools, nor did he have materials.

During his third pass alongside the rim the young man paused a moment at a particularly narrow section of the ravine. Large pine trees stood on either side, their roots partially exposed within the gorge. It was these roots that had limited the damage of the raging water as it rushed down the mountain. The chasm was still too wide to jump, but Nikos wondered whether he could somehow construct a small bridge to connect the little ledges formed by the roots.

Once again the young man sat down, but this time with purpose and resolve. Studying the roots of the two trees, he found several places where they emerged from the sides of the gorge and the tops of the ledges. The roots appeared to be limber and firmly attached to the trees, both of which were still alive. That much engendered hope.

Nikos narrowed his focus to the far side. His eyes skipped from one root to another until they fell on one particularly promising one. Not only was it substantial enough to support his weight, but its end turned upward, forming a natural hook. Now if he could only find a way to connect that hook to his side of the gorge....

The young man sprang to his feet abruptly. Although he did not have the tools and material to build a proper bridge, he did have a way to construct a primitive one. The answer was around his waist, holding his robe neatly in place! He unfastened his fabric girdle, and as he did, the fold that had hung over his girdle disappeared. Almost immediately his robe billowed and fluttered in the breeze, as if protesting the indignity. Nikos did not care. He knew what to do now, and he worked quickly.

First he tore his girdle into strips. Next he found some sturdy, yet still supple branches at least a pace longer than the width of the chasm. After aligning the boughs on the ground, he wove the strips of girdle in and out through the limbs. Soon it became clear, though, that he would run out of strips long before he could finish the job!

Nikos slumped down in frustration and anger. "Why can't anything just be easy?" he demanded, as though the mountain itself might acknowledge his dilemma. There was no answer.

No solution came to mind as the young man sat, brooding and generally feeling sorry for himself, but that all changed when a breeze suddenly grabbed the hem of his robe, causing it to flutter wildly. At that moment, Nikos realized that he had limited himself to his sash, but that he could easily tear additional strips of fabric from the end of his robe.

Working with renewed fervor, the young man soon had enough fabric strips to complete his bridge. His robe no longer flowed to his ankles, but stopped just below his knees. A jagged edge had replaced an orderly hem, which flapped defiantly with every puff of wind. Nikos did not care.

The young man wove the new strips in and out through the limbs, as he had with the strips from the girdle. Finally, Nikos formed a small loop with the last strip of fabric, securing it to one end of his crude project.

Prior to hauling his little bridge down onto the ledge closest to him, the young man looked around for a rock he could use as a hammer and some broken pieces of branches that would work as pegs. He found his hammer and pegs quickly, tossing them onto the primitive structure before lifting one end of it.

Nikos dragged it over the rim of the chasm with a grunt, then concentrated on preventing the bridge from sliding farther down the slope on its own. Allowing gravity to do most of the work, the young man positioned his creation at the edge of the vertical drop from the cluster of roots on his side of the ravine. Standing the bridge on end, he lowered it into position with the loop over the hooked root on the far side. Then he tugged at his side of the bridge, placed his homemade pegs in position, and hammered them down with a few quick blows from the rock. The bridge was done!

He was proud of himself, but at the same time, doubtful. Would the bridge hold? He pushed at it gently. The structure swayed slightly, but seemed stable. That test gave him courage for the next trial. He put one foot out onto his creation, slowly shifting his weight. As he did, the bridge pitched to the right and he almost lost his balance. Nikos jerked his foot back quickly, his heart suddenly racing and his lungs greedily sucking in air. Clearly, walking across was too dangerous.

The young man stood still at one end of his homemade bridge, pausing a moment to regain his composure and to summon his courage. He was mere steps from the other side, but even closer to an ugly accident – maybe even death. Looking down into the trench, Nikos imagined his body bouncing from one side to the other, limply drawing a legion of rocks and pebbles behind it until finally settling into a grotesque posture at the bottom. For a brief moment, he considered turning back.

"No!" he howled, startling himself. His voice echoed through the miniature canyon, as though even the mountain mocked him. "I'm crossing!" he declared to himself. "And I'm going now."

Nikos sat down, legs straddling either side of the bridge and crossing underneath it. Bending forward, he reached with both arms to clutch the edges of his creation. Hands gripped, arms heaved, and legs pushed, propelling the young man across even as the bridge twisted and shook and rolled. Progress was slow, but steady. Finally, the determined young man grasped the upturned root at the far side and yanked himself onto the ledge. He had made it!

Scrambling to the top, Nikos looked back. It was a moment to catch his breath, but more than that, it was a moment to relish his victory. What had presented itself as impossible wasn't, and what had almost made him turn back didn't. He had vanquished the obstacle that had filled him with dread! He turned his back on the ravine, once again headed up the mountain.

To compensate for lost time, the young man picked up his pace, even trotting on parts of the trail that were fairly level. He did not mind the exertion now—he was still exhilarated by victory. The remainder of his trek up the mountain was uneventful, and it passed quickly. Soon he found himself at the path that diverged toward the home of his teacher.

Turning onto the path, Nikos bounded up the ugly granite

steps and trotted through the barren canopy of tree limbs and tangled vines, eventually emerging into the meadow where he had seen the abandoned log building. As he came into the clearing, he saw Mediocrates.

His mentor stood close to the odd building with his back to Nikos, apparently examining the structure. The old philosopher leaned on a gnarled and knotted staff. As the young man drew within a dozen paces, Mediocrates turned.

"It's about time you showed up!" he groused. "And what a sight you are," he added, pointing accusingly toward Nikos's free-flowing robe.

"The trail was washed out," the still exuberant disciple explained. "So I built a bridge." He uttered the last sentence with satisfaction. His statement was an expression of pride rather than an excuse for being late.

"Humpf!"

Mediocrates turned his back on Nikos, once again facing the dilapidated building. As he did, the young man realized that he had never once seen his mentor in a positive frame of mind. True, the old man had smiled on more than one occasion, but never from contentment. In fact, the smiles were really sneers. Evidently, joy was not part of the life of the old philosopher.

"What do you see here?" Mediocrates snapped, impatient for this lesson to be done.

Stepping up to the structure, Nikos examined it quickly before answering. "I can see that the roof is complete, as is the western wall, but the other walls were left undone. From the aging, I believe at least 10 years have passed since anyone worked on it. Do you know what this is, and why work stopped?"

"I'll ask the questions!" Mediocrates snarled. His mood this day was particularly unpleasant, and his manner and tone obnoxious. "Why do *you* suppose construction stopped?" he retorted, stressing the word *you* viciously.

"I don't know," Nikos replied calmly, not allowing his mentor's foul mood to upset him. "Perhaps the builder was called away, or perhaps he fell ill. Maybe he died."

"Do you see anything here that tells the story?" the old man prodded, ignoring his student's conjectures. "Look carefully."

Nikos studied the structure, first with his eyes, then with hands that ran along the logs. Nothing caught his attention. The young man glanced toward his teacher, recognizing right away that the old philosopher expected him to keep searching, so he resumed his examination. He walked around the structure slowly and deliberately, trying to observe everything. Still nothing! Mediocrates watched in impatient silence.

"I've looked over every log and every peg," Nikos finally asserted in desperation. "I see no clue to tell me why the builder abandoned it."

Stretching his arm in the direction of one of the incomplete walls, Mediocrates extended his forefinger toward a rusted piece of metal lying half buried. "What about that?" he asked. There was a trace of resentment in his voice.

Nikos took a couple of steps toward the object and stooped over to pick it up. The piece of metal remained firmly embedded in the ground that long ago claimed it. Getting onto his knees, the young man dug around the object, then used both hands to pry it loose. It resisted at first, but then capitulated without warning. The young man's efforts to yank the object from the ground had succeeded, though at the cost of planting his posterior on the rock-hard clay.

Mediocrates snickered spitefully. "What do you have there, young man?"

His disciple sat up to take a better look at the object. Although much of the blade had been broken off, and rust had further marred the form and dulled the edge, Nikos could clearly see what the thing had once been. "It looks like an old axe head," he answered. "It's not much use now, though."

"What can you surmise from that?" Mediocrates prodded. "Why would an axe head be there in the ground?"

"Perhaps it came off the handle," the young man answered. "But that doesn't really explain anything," he added, wondering what direction his teacher would take.

"Of course it does!" Mediocrates wore a feigned look of astonishment that Nikos recognized immediately. "The story is so obvious. How can you not see it?" he asked, shaking his head. A grand sweep of his left arm toward the building site served as a dramatic introduction to his next question. "How do you suppose these logs were shaped?"

"Probably with an axe," the young man replied. "Maybe even this one."

"And what does that tell you about the state of this building?"

Nikos was annoyed by this game. "I have no idea! Are you planning to tell me, or do you intend to take a nap first?" The irritation in the pupil's voice was evident in his first statement, but the allusion to their previous meeting in the second statement made it clear that the young man was no longer easily intimidated by the old philosopher.

Mediocrates grimaced at his protégé's slur. Inspecting Nikos's face, the old man saw an assurance he had not seen before. He did not like the young man's newfound strength, nor did he appreciate the insult. He decided to make a note of the first and to overlook the second.

"We have an axe head," he stated matter-of-factly, "but its

cutting edge has been broken off. Clearly, as you yourself said, it's no longer of any use." The old philosopher looked expectantly at his pupil.

Nikos sighed, knowing that Mediocrates would not say more until he had a response of some sort from the young man. "Perhaps the workman injured himself," he proposed without any enthusiasm. "Or maybe he just tired of the project."

"Why would he quit after so much work?" The philosopher's question was straightforward, resurrecting the young man's interest. "There are two possibilities," the old man began, suspending his thought in mid-sentence for effect and carefully watching his student for a reaction.

The young man's mind sifted through a throng of ideas that presented themselves as legitimate contenders. None made any real sense; all were imposters.

"Two possibilities show themselves," Mediocrates said slowly and emphatically, "assuming the authoritative posture he so often wore.

Nikos stood, momentarily perplexed but also determined to answer. "The builder either quit on his own," the young man blurted out, "or he was forced to quit!"

"Exactly!" Mediocrates uttered this single word smugly. It was less an acknowledgment of his disciple's answer than it was an expression of his own satisfaction at having guided the young man to this understanding. "Now what can you surmise from the axe head?"

"The builder quit because the head broke," Nikos replied. "But that still does not explain why he never replaced the axe so he could resume his work."

The old man stiffened at the second statement. "You're moving along too quickly," he scolded, his tone as sharp as the piercing stare directed at his pupil. "Which possibility commends itself to you as more plausible? Did the builder simply quit, or was he forced to quit?"

Bearing in mind the unexpectedly emotional response of his mentor, Nikos considered the options presented to him. Perhaps Mediocrates was the builder who quit. That possibility would explain his defensiveness, and that possibility suggested the choice the young man should choose.

"He was forced to quit," the pupil said obediently, "because the blade broke."

"Yes, yes!" Mediocrates exclaimed, gleeful at this validation of his own opinion. "And since he never returned to continue work," the old man continued in an excited flurry of words, "he obviously had no way to replace the axe. Circumstances forced him to abandon the project."

Nikos stood before his master, quietly doubting, and finally asking, "Why would it be so difficult to replace an axe?"

In a flash the demeanor of his teacher changed from gleeful self-satisfaction to enraged insolence. "Exactly how would someone on this mountain replace an axe?" he demanded. "What tools would he use to create a new blade? Where would he obtain the right materials? Where would he find a forge?" Both the rapidity and the intensity of this barrage stunned Nikos.

"I'm not sure," he replied, almost as a whisper. "Couldn't he just hike down to Pouthena to have one made by the...."

"What makes you think the builder would have wanted to enter that nauseating little community?" Mediocrates interrupted, vomiting his words with an anger Nikos had not yet seen. The young man stood, unsure how to respond. After an uncomfortable silence, Mediocrates sheathed his anger, composing himself just enough to finish for the day.

"That brings us to the point of today's lesson," the old philosopher grunted. "Life is hard, and it's mean. When it places insurmountable obstacles in your way, you're better off turning around. You'll save yourself lots of aggravation and frustration."

Lifting his chin in a haughty pose, Mediocrates spun around and stomped off.

CHAPTER 10

AN ANSWER FOUND

N ikos worked his way through the stalls and booths of the agora, breathing heavily as a result of the pack on his back. He had made the trip up the trail from the harbor five times today, beginning at daybreak. It was now mid-afternoon, and he was thankful that this load was to be his last. He still had time to wander through the agora, perusing the assortment of goods on display, but also watching the spectacle of *trading day.*

Pouthena had its regular merchants whose emporia were open every day, but the monthly *trading day* brought in merchants—and shoppers—from the villages and smaller towns in the region. On those days, the agora transformed itself into a riot of noise and color. Traders erected elaborate booths and colorful tents wherever space permitted, creating a haphazard maze for throngs of buyers. Hawkers generated an energy of their own as they pushed their way through the maze, jumping in front of anyone who happened to glance in their direction for a moment.

Village traders brought wools and produce, and even

livestock, from nearby farms. Craftsmen from towns in the region brought their best ceramic jugs and pots, jewelry, and leather goods to display. Pouthena's own merchants offered many of the same things, but also featured ivory and linen and spices shipped from faraway ports with exotic names. Nikos loved *trading day*!

"Spiros, Spiros, come quickly!" The words raced past Nikos's ears, but not before drawing his eyes toward their source. The woman, now standing at the entrance to Alexandros's emporium, waved excitedly toward someone behind Nikos. Though framed by gray wisps of unruly hair, her features reflected an almost child-like delight. Somehow her movements expressed both the dignity of her years and the joy of the moment.

"I've found the answer," she yelped enthusiastically.

Nikos, who had paused to take in this scene, turned to see the object of her discourse. A balding man approached briskly. Anticipation wrestled with caution for mastery of his face.

"Are you sure, Xenia?"

"Come and see for yourself!" The thrill in her tone, unusual even for trading day, piqued Nikos's curiosity. He decided to follow the two into Alexandros's emporium so he could see the *answer* for himself. The young man waited for Spiros to pass, and then followed, carefully maintaining a respectful distance while staying close enough to hear.

"Here it is! Here, Spiros!" The words burst out of Xenia's mouth as soon as she reached an enormous ceramic pot. She was breathing heavily, but from excitement rather than exertion.

Her husband arrived moments later, carefully examining her discovery. "It's just an ordinary pot," he objected, "except for this hole close to the base. How will this thing solve our problem?"

"It's called a *clepsydra**." The friendly, confident voice was one Nikos knew well. It was the voice of Alexandros, the

---

* *Water Thief* in Greek

proprietor for whom the young man had traversed the distance between harbor and agora five times today.

Spiros eyed the pot warily, finally putting his finger into the hole as though doing so would help him understand its purpose. The finger failed to shed light on the mystery. "What good is a pot with a hole in its side?" he asked abruptly, looking directly into Alexandros's face.

"Big cities use the *water thief* to set limits on the time people may speak in public debates," the merchant replied. "The pot always empties in the same amount of time."

"That's fine for large cities," Spiros asserted, unhappy with the answer. "We have nothing to time on our farm. I see no way that a jug with a hole in its side can be of any use to us!" He shook his head dramatically, as though to declare that further discussion would be foolish.

"Spiros—let the man finish," his wife pleaded. To the casual observer, her words were soft and unassuming, an entreaty that evoked pity. To the balding man who had spent his life with her, the words said much more. They hinted at her disappointment. He turned back toward the pot and Xenia, as well as the proprietor.

"I certainly understand your feelings," Alexandros continued, still exuding a pleasant confidence. Nikos had often witnessed this man turn doubts into hope and distrust into anticipation with nothing more than words.

"You clearly do not need a timer," Alexandros added. "What you do need, though, is a way to water your garden without washing the tender young plants down the hillside. Is that right?"

"Yes," Spiros admitted, unsure how this merchant standing before him knew the problem that had vexed him so long.

"Xenia described your problem to me on trading day two months ago," Alexandros explained, realizing by the hesitant tone of the man's voice that Xenia had never told him about that conversation. "I promised then that I would do my best to find a solution."

"But how does a timer do that?" The old farmer's voice reflected a subdued frustration that had displaced the disappointment he had displayed just moments before. He waited, looking into the eyes of the merchant without any real hope of an answer that would satisfy him.

"This *water thief* achieves its purpose by regulating the flow of water," Alexandros replied. "You need a stream of water sufficient to irrigate your garden, but not so robust as to destroy it. The answer lies in controlling the flow. And that is precisely what a *water thief* does."

"See, Spiros? This is what we need!" The older woman's voice had lost none of its former enthusiasm, but now reflected a warmth intended to reassure her husband.

"How fast does the water flow?" he asked with budding eagerness. "Is this the only one you have? Are there different sizes? Do any flow at different rates?" The questions began bursting out of his mouth in rapid succession, displaying a newfound zeal for this solution.

His curiosity satisfied, Nikos headed to the back of the emporium to unload his pack. As he did, he marveled at Alexandros's talent for coming up with the ideal product for each of his many customers. This incident was not the first time Nikos had witnessed Alexandros's ingenuity. Each time the young man saw an exchange of this sort, he mulled it over in his mind, but had not yet been able to figure out the question so many of Pouthena's residents asked themselves. "How does he do it?"

After unloading his pack and organizing the items in the back room, the young man started toward the front door, intent on enjoying the remnants of *trading day*. Looking around, Nikos realized that Spiros and Xenia had already left. In fact, no customers were in the emporium.

The young man spun around on impulse. Walking straight up to Alexandros, Nikos asked the question that had been on his mind.

"Sir? How do you always have the perfect products on hand?"

Alexandros smiled, gazing intently at his young friend. "I don't, actually," he said, turning his attention back to a leather harness on one of his shelves. Without any real purpose, he fiddled with the harness, waiting for Nikos's response.

The merchant's answer puzzled the young man. Half a dozen times in as many weeks Nikos had witnessed Alexandros selling some unique item to an exultant customer. Long before the young man had begun working at the emporium, and long before he had seen this talent for himself, he had heard the envious comments of other merchants.

"Well, you did today!"

Looking up suddenly, while putting the harness down on the shelf, Alexandros studied his young worker. "Not exactly," he replied slowly and thoughtfully. "It's true, I had the *clepsydra* today, and I sold it to Spiros and Xenia, who were very happy."

"Then I'm right," Nikos contended, missing the stress placed on the word *today*.

"Do you think the *water thief* magically appeared in my inventory?"

"No sir, but you had it right when you needed it."

"That's true," Alexandros agreed. "But I didn't have it the first time Xenia came to me. That was a couple of months ago. Do you remember when I acquired it? You should—you were the one who brought it up from the harbor!"

"Yes, that was just a couple of weeks ago," Nikos admitted. "But how did you know about the *water thief*? And how did you know it would work for Spiros and Xenia?"

"I didn't know for sure then. What I did know was their problem. Do you know why?"

The question surprised Nikos. He had considered the possibility that Alexandros might not share his secret, but he had not anticipated a line of questions that he would have to answer.

"The old woman told you. At least, that's what you seemed to be saying earlier."

"And that's my secret!" Alexandros exclaimed with a big grin. "That's the secret everyone wants to know!"

"What's the secret?" the young man asked, mystified at his employer's statement and confused by his demeanor. "I don't understand."

"Nikos, it's really quite simple. What did I do to learn the problem that vexed Spiros and Xenia?"

"Listen to her, I guess."

"Exactly!" Alexandros cried out, still smiling. As he did, he placed his hand on Nikos's shoulder.

Nikos endeavored to understand where Alexandros was going with his reasoning. How could listening be the secret to Alexandros's success? The effort showed on his face, prompting the merchant to continue.

"I learned a long time ago that it's much easier to sell something a buyer really wants than to persuade that same individual to purchase something I happen to think is great," he noted. "And how do you suppose I learn what buyers want?"

"You listen?"

"Exactly."

"That still doesn't explain how you always have the right

product at the right time!" Nikos spoke passionately, but respectfully. He was frustrated, but admiration for Alexandros tempered that frustration.

"You're right," the merchant acknowledged. "Listening is the first step. Before I can move on, though, I need to explain what real listening is. Are you willing to listen, young man?"

"Yes, sir," Nikos agreed, recognizing in his employer's question a mild rebuke.

"You listen," Alexandros continued, "but not merely to the words. You must understand what's in the heart. Only then can you truly comprehend the problem. Does this make sense?"

"I think so."

"I'm not sure you do—let me explain. Customers don't always understand their own problems. My task is to uncover the real issues, usually by asking questions. Only then can I help my customers solve their problems."

"Okay, I see that it's important to understand the problem first," Nikos interjected. "What I still don't understand is how you always come up with the right answers."

"Nikos, I *don't* always come up with the right answers," the old merchant explained with a laugh. "However, I do admit to frequent success," he added, a big grin still testifying to his delight at the young man's statement.

"Alright," Nikos replied, also smiling. "How do you come up with the right answers so frequently?" He exaggerated the last two words, conceding his previous error, but at the same time, insisting on the validity of his question.

"That's the interesting part," Alexandros replied. "Just as there's an art to listening, there's an art to finding solutions. To put it bluntly, look somewhere else!"

"Where?"

Reading the confusion in his employee's expression, Alexandros followed up his enigmatic statement with another question. "How would you solve a problem, young man?"

Nikos thought a moment, then responded. "First, I'd find out how other people had tackled the same problem."

"And then?"

"I'd do what they did." The answer was half-hearted. The young man knew Alexandros wasn't asking him how to solve everyday problems, but problems that seemed to have no solution. At the moment, though, he wasn't sure how else to answer.

"Suppose that doesn't work. Would you give up?"

Nikos remembered his last lesson with Mediocrates. The grumpy philosopher had advocated turning away from "insurmountable obstacles." Clearly, that was not Alexandros's approach.

"I wouldn't want to," the young man offered. "But I don't know. I don't know."

"I'm glad you wouldn't want to quit," Alexandros proclaimed. "Suppose I tell you that there's a way to think about difficult problems that will help you solve more of them. Would you want to know that method?"

"Yes!"

"Then look somewhere else!"

"You said that before. What do you mean?"

"Xenia told me that she and Spiros had talked to at least a dozen merchants in the towns and villages close by, but no one had come up with an answer that would work. When someone tells me that dozens of merchants couldn't solve a problem, I know to look somewhere else for the answer. Do you understand?"

"I think so."

Alexandros could see his worker was open to learning more, though he had not yet fully grasped the concept. "Spiros and Xenia never would have come to me if a standard approach had worked," the old merchant continued. "So I thought about the problem, which in their case was their hillside. It's so steep that standard irrigation washes their garden away. They needed a way to slow the flow of water. Once I identified the real problem—the rate of flow—I looked elsewhere for the answer."

"But how did you discover the *water thief*?"

"By looking in a way that most people never do," Alexandros sighed. "When you look at the world, LOOK!" Don't just walk by, ignoring everything. Look at everything."

"How will that help?"

"As you look, consider how things work, and why," Alexandros continued. "Then, when you've practicing looking as long as I have, you'll not only understand the people around you, but you'll see answers everywhere!"

The merchant's approach was beginning to make sense to the young man. Nikos had always enjoyed watching people, but he had never thought of that activity as productive. He smiled at the idea that something so simple could be so powerful.

"When did you discover the *water thief*?" Nikos asked, still curious.

"I was still a young man, perhaps a couple of years older than you are now. In those days I traveled with my father to some of the big cities a couple of times a year. He was always looking for items that our townspeople would need."

As Alexandros spoke, the weight of years seemed to disappear from his frame. Although Nikos had never seen the merchant without a smile, he seemed particularly buoyant as he began to recount this experience from so long ago.

"It was always so exciting," he continued, reliving the wonder of youth. "The day I discovered a *water thief* was the day of a great debate among the citizens of the city we were visiting. It was all new to me, and even my father seemed intrigued. I no longer remember what the citizens were discussing, but I remember how they spoke with great passion and energy as they raced to finish their remarks before the *clepsydra* could empty its contents."

"What made you think it would solve the problem Xenia brought you?" Nikos asked abruptly, snapping Alexandros from his narrative.

"I've never forgotten that moment so many years ago. It was an exciting discovery then and it's a pleasant memory now. Do you know why it was so exciting?"

"Because it was new to you?" Nikos offered.

"Partly," Alexandros replied. "What was most exciting, though, is that I learned. After the debate concluded, I asked the citizens there as many questions as I could. I wanted to know how the *water thief* worked and why they used it. They were amused, and asked me whether I planned to host a debate, but I didn't care. I wanted to know."

"None of this tells me what made you think of the *water thief* as a solution," Nikos protested.

"I'm getting there," the merchant chuckled. "Let an old man enjoy his memories. And as for you, young man, try listening more." Alexandros paused a moment to drive his point home.

Nikos nodded and waited.

"The most difficult part of looking somewhere else," Alexandros began with a slight sigh, "is training your heart not to prevent your mind from seeing the answer right in front of you."

The young man looked at his employer, but said nothing. He

simply waited.

"To be successful, you've got to take the answer from one setting and put it into another," the old man explained. "At first your heart will protest, but don't let it stop you!"

Nikos sat still, mulling over the strategy.

"Oh, and one more thing. You probably won't find the answer in the first item you take from one environment to place in another. You may have to consider dozens of potential solutions."

CHAPTER 11

GARDEN IN CHAOS

Approaching a cluster of juniper trees, Nikos hesitated a moment, then turned around. The sun had not yet broken the horizon, but had already painted its purple canvas with streaks of pink and blue. The young man silently waited, not so much for the sunlight that would make his journey easier, but to gather his resolve. Somehow, he thought, the brightness of a new day would give him that strength.

The trek up the mountain today would be his sixth. Previous trips in brisk wind or in bitter cold, in thick fog or in freezing rain, had given Nikos an appreciation for the perils. He had come to know the trail, but more important, he had come to know more about the old man who lived halfway up the mountain. With that knowledge came fatigue, of heart more than of body.

He again looked at the eastern sky, where pinks and blues were disappearing with the brilliance of dawn. Reluctantly, Nikos turned back toward the junipers that had marked the boundary of his boyhood adventures. Still weary in spirit, he set out to meet Mediocrates.

Rounding the junipers and starting up the mountain, the

young man considered his mentor. An aura of mystery had surrounded the philosopher when student first encountered master, but each successive meeting with the bitter old man had worn away the mystery. In its place was a growing emptiness Nikos dreaded. That emptiness, as much as the dangers of the trail, had wearied the young man.

All morning Nikos had been of two minds. At times he was ready to forego the journey, abandoning his lessons with the grizzled old philosopher and renouncing their relationship. At other times, though, he thought beyond the immediate, considering what he would tell friends who knew what he had been up to all along. Worst of all was the thought of admitting to Penelope that she was right.

The young man loved Penelope. She was the only mother he had ever known, and she had always done everything in her power to nurture and guide him. Now that Nikos was at the cusp of manhood, the nurturing and guidance were often irritants, continually reminding him that he was not yet a real man. He desperately wanted to make his own way in the world, and he wanted Penelope to see him as a man rather than the orphaned boy she had adopted.

These thoughts propelled the weary young man this morning, first wrenching him from bed, then driving him to the edge of town, and now hurling him onto the mountain path. Even so, his feet seemed particularly heavy as he tramped along the now-familiar track. Placing one foot in front of the other methodically, he moved up the mountain without any real passion. Nikos's head hung from his shoulders, face down, allowing him to eye the heartless rhythm playing out at the ends of his legs.

The path almost doubled back on itself, following the contour of a finger of land jutting from the mountainside. This switchback was the first in a parade of more than a dozen sharp angles and sudden turns. Each mocked the solitary hiker with the suggestion that he had already been there this morning, and that he was making no progress. Nikos pushed on.

By the time the young man had reached the fifteenth switchback, the crispness of morning had retreated from the onslaught of the sun. Patches of shade from trees near the trail offered only momentary relief from an overhead adversary bent on punishing him. Nikos kept walking, quickly putting out of his mind thoughts of cold ale and tall tales among friends at the Square.

Had the young man been reclining in the shade at any one of dozens of points along the track, the day would have presented opportunities to enjoy the stunning vistas below. Nikos thought about Melissa, trying unsuccessfully to put his special friend out of mind. He imagined the two of them sharing a lazy lunch on one of these grassy spots. As he did, and knowing those moments must wait, he almost resented the splendor of forested hills backed by the gleaming blue of the sea beyond.

Fortunately, the trail turned, and with it, his eyes. A more ordinary picture of scrub trees and rocky terrain before him allowed Nikos to focus on the day's objective, unhindered by fleeting dreams and whispered yearnings. A distinctive boulder came into view, letting the young man know that he was drawing close to the spot where the path widened. Just beyond was the bridge he had created using nothing more than strips of fabric and branches. He smiled at the thought of the little victory he enjoyed that day.

Nikos's demeanor changed after he remembered that success and how it made him feel at the time. His head no longer hung from his shoulders and his eyes no longer kept watch over plodding feet. Straightening his torso, the hiker pushed ahead with greater vigor.

Suddenly he was at the little bridge. Carefully climbing down the ledge bordering the gorge, the young man looked around him. Nothing seemed to have changed much since he had been here a month before, returning from his last meeting with the old philosopher. A few striations marked new channels in which water flowed, testifying to at least one rain shower since his last trip. These traces of erosion, however, were minor. Clearly, the preceding month had seen no downpour as torrential as the one that had formed the gorge.

Stepping up to the bridge, Nikos tested it with his foot. It swayed slightly, but felt as secure as it had been the day he completed it. The young man squatted next to his creation, and then sat down, hanging both feet over the ledge. Preparing to cross as he had the previous month, he put his legs on either side of the structure and brought them together underneath. He reached forward with both hands to grasp interwoven branches and fabric. Pausing, he breathed slowly and deeply, and then began. He was on the other side moments later.

The young man continued his journey, but noticed that all sense of dread had vanished. Uneasiness had given way to quiet reflection, and weariness had yielded to a sense of purpose. Merely walking, and then crossing his little bridge, had finally driven out the darkness of his earlier mood. Nikos began to enjoy the day's climb. The sky seemed bluer, the trees greener, and the air fresher. Even the rhythm of his feet seemed livelier.

As the thoughtful hiker progressed, he studied the trail. There was much that was familiar, but much he had never noticed. Perhaps the wind and fog and slush of previous treks had forced him to focus solely on the path itself. Today, however, the way did not seem so treacherous, so he looked around as he continued. The ground on his right-hand side frequently fell away dramatically, creating steep slopes that would have been extremely difficult to climb. What struck Nikos, though, is how many of these slopes were populated by trees, bent and disfigured by the wind, clinging tenaciously to their perches.

The young man drew close to the location of his first meeting with Mediocrates. Once again the trail narrowed, and once again the solitary hiker felt the attack of rocks, ruts, and roots on his feet. This time Nikos noticed the source of those roots. Several gnarled and stunted oaks lined the ridge of the slope, holding it in place against the onslaught of rain and wind. He stopped for a moment, impressed with the persistence of these guardians of the path. The same roots he had despised on earlier trips were the ones that held the trail open for him and anyone else willing to make this climb. Those roots weren't enemies, after all. In a way, they were allies in the campaign against this mountain.

"You won't find any truths buried among those roots," a familiar voice called, as though privy to the young man's thoughts. "Besides, it's past time for us to begin your next lesson." Mediocrates emerged from a cluster of trees wearing what passed for a smile. It was really more of a self-satisfied grin, but it was the closest the old philosopher had ever come to smiling in Nikos's presence.

The young man left the trail and its protective roots, happy that his mentor appeared to be in a better frame of mind than usual. He closed the distance to his teacher with a dozen brisk steps. Once he had reached the white-haired philosopher, Nikos waited.

"I have something to show you," the old man said. "Follow me." The words were matter-of-fact, but hinted at something pleasing to Mediocrates. He turned around, setting off at a pace at odds with his usual bearing. Student labored to keep up with master. Finally, their jaunt along the path to the old man's home ended.

"What do you think?" he asked, sweeping his arm in a grand gesture to draw the young man's attention to a plot of recently excavated earth. Among the jumble of leaves and shoots, Nikos recognized onion and garlic plants. He also noticed a cucumber vine that had worked itself into a tangle with chick peas.

"I'm not sure," Nikos responded, carefully choosing his words. He had learned not to speak too quickly when replying to the old philosopher's queries. "I would guess this is your garden."

"Your conjecture is correct," the white-haired gardener affirmed. "Do you notice anything distinctive about it?"

The young man shifted uncomfortably, hoping to come up with truthful but inoffensive words to describe the chaotic array of plants, and he hoped to do so before Mediocrates pounced on him. No such words came to mind.

"Have you no answer, young man?" The old man's tone had changed. "Do you have eyes? Or do you hold me in such contempt that you won't give me an answer?"

"No sir!" the young man declared defensively. "It's just that I wanted to choose the right words."

"Is it so hard for you to tell me your thoughts? I'm not asking for something difficult. I'm asking for *your thoughts*, not someone else's." The words spewed out of the old man's mouth like boiling water erupting from a cauldron.

"I'm sorry," Nikos muttered, looking at his feet. "The garden appears to be somewhat overgrown, as though you haven't spent much time maintaining it."

"Precisely!" Mediocrates bellowed, as though he had just

achieved a great victory. "I've spent very little time maintaining this garden." A smug and condescending smile materialized with this pronouncement. The philosopher allowed a moment to pass in silence, heightening the tension between teacher and pupil.

Nikos said nothing. He had grown accustomed to the old man's techniques, and so he merely waited for his mentor to continue.

"What would you presume to be the advantages—or disadvantages—of my style of gardening?"

The young man once again shifted, as though he could displace some of the discomfort he felt when confronted by the old man's double-edged questions. "I can think of no advantages, but several disadvantages occur to me. Your cucumber vine is strangling your chick peas, and your onions and garlic are struggling to grow among weeds. Your yield will be considerably smaller than it might have been had you tended to them a bit more."

"That's exactly the prosaic manner of thinking I would expect from someone down in Pouthena!" Mediocrates complained. "I had hoped that by this time you would have embraced a more highly developed approach to life!"

Nikos was proud of his community, and he loved its people. To hear Mediocrates ridicule them irked him. "Suppose you enlighten me, then," he snapped.

An angry glare flashed across the philosopher's face, but quickly disappeared. In its place was an insincere smile. "Ah, yes, I guess I have pushed you too hard and too fast," he said, almost as though making a mental note to himself. "Do you suppose I'll harvest nothing from my garden," he asked with a pretense of apprehension.

"No, I'm sure you'll reap a crop," Nikos replied, realizing that his mentor was asking questions not to discover answers, but to direct the young man's thinking. "However, your yield won't be as bountiful as it could have been," he added, defending his initial response.

"So in your mind it's not a matter of whether I'll harvest, but of how much?" Mediocrates stared into the soul of his student.

Nikos reluctantly nodded in agreement with the old man's analysis.

"Would you be so kind as to tell me how much of a difference?" the philosopher asked in a slightly more provocative tone. "No need to be precise," he added. "An estimate will be fine."

"I don't really know," the young man murmured. "The rain, the soil, and the sun make a big difference in your yield," he added, scrambling for an answer that made sense. "Keeping the weeds down and directing the growth of vines matter, though." Nikos knew that without specifics, he had already lost the battle.

Mediocrates cast a sour look at his pupil, then assaulted him from another direction. "Would you say that maintaining my garden should take precedence over everything else?"

"No, not everything," the young man replied, unsure why his mentor had changed his approach.

"Exactly!" The word exploded from the philosopher's mouth, leaving behind a smug smile. "Then you agree that maintaining my garden is not that important?" Mediocrates asserted, assuming the mantle of victory.

"I didn't say that," Nikos objected, realizing too late that the old man had tricked him. "Just because some things may be more important does not mean the garden is unimportant."

"Don't quibble with words, young man! My point stands." The old man shuffled over to a nearby tree stump, turned around, and plopped down.

"If I allowed that garden to take over my life, where would I be?" Without waiting for his pupil to answer, the old man continued. "I'd be worn out, and I'd have no time for anything else. Hardly a fair exchange for another handful of onions and cucumbers!"

Nikos stood quietly, considering his mentor's contention.

"This brings us to our next rule," Mediocrates declared in his most authoritative tone.

Nikos drew closer, waiting for the old man to speak again.

"Don't invite unnecessary anxiety into your life after you've started a project. You've done the hard part—starting. So relax a little, allow yourself to attend to other matters, and your project will take care of itself."

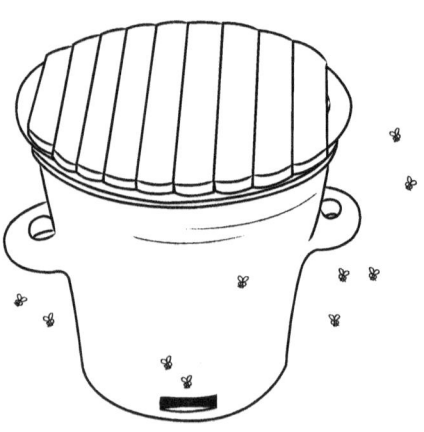

CHAPTER 12

GOLDEN HARVEST

Carrying the pungent, yet still pleasant scent of smoldering pine knots, the afternoon breeze confirmed to Nikos that Melissa was in the back working with her bees. Skirting along the edge of her little cottage, the young man bounded down a path he had traveled many times.

Melissa was more than a friend to Nikos. They had grown up together, playing on the Magistrate's Steps or running through the crowds on trading days. They had explored the fields and woods encircling Pouthena, and they had splashed across the harbor bay to claim bragging rights as the faster swimmer.

For the past few months, though, everything seemed different. Whenever the young man's eyes chanced upon Melissa's auburn hair, his chest felt too small for his heart. Hearing her voice, or catching sight of her, brought a smile to his face that attested to the thrill in his soul. For months Melissa had never been far from his thoughts.

After winding through a thicket mostly populated by pines and laurels, the path emerged into an opening overlooking the sea and harbor below. A legion of pale gray-green leaves in neat rows greeted the young man with the unmistakable woody aroma of thyme. Surrounded on the north, west, and southwest by walls of pine and laurel, and to the east and southeast by a sheer rock cliff, the opening provided a pleasant, peaceful haven for Melissa to work with her bees.

During the past few months, this private paradise had also become a haven for Nikos. He stepped into the opening, breathless because of his pace, but also breathless at the sight of Melissa. For a moment, he simply stood. She had her back to him, but he did not call her name. Instead, he studied her form. In the same way that he could never ignore a sunset, or tear his eyes away from a fire on a frosty night, Nikos found himself powerless to turn away.

Turning slightly, Melissa soon realized she was not alone. She spun around completely, then saw who was in the clearing with her.

"I didn't think I'd see you today," she stated, hiding her delight behind a friendly, but restrained, demeanor. For the auburn-haired young woman, waiting for Nikos to make up his mind was the most difficult part of their *friendship*. They had always been good friends, but she was ready for more. And so was he, judging from the many times lately she had caught him staring at her!

"Alexandros sent me," Nikos said, as though business was his only reason to stop by.

"That's funny." Melissa's terse statement trailed off, as though she had no real interest in expressing her thoughts, and yet compelling a response from the breathless young man standing in her bee yard.

"What's funny?" he asked, a little bewildered. Even as he had grown more enamored by his life-long friend, she had become more distant. They used to tell each other everything, but not anymore. He wanted to tell her how he felt, and that he thought about her continually, but he couldn't say anything until he understood what was behind her growing indifference.

"It's funny that you're out of breath," she said. "Alexandros must be in a real hurry!" she added, her tone abruptly transforming from thoughtful detachment into mild sarcasm.

Nikos winced a little, still not sure why Melissa was acting this way. "No, Alexandros simply told me to stop by for some fresh thyme," he admitted. "I thought if I ran here, I would have more time to spend with you." The words were honest, but Melissa detected more. There was a hint of defeat in Nikos's admission that made it impossible for her to continue her cynical remarks.

"Well let's make the most of our time!" Springing across the opening, Melissa hugged the confused young man, barely finishing her sentence before reaching him. The leap from sarcasm to enthusiasm was more startling, sweeping defeat aside and ushering in new hope.

"I want to show you something," she said, grabbing his hand and pulling him forward. Nothing could have prevented his broad smile. The warmth of Melissa's hand, the heady fragrance of thyme mingled with smoke from pine knots, the brilliant amber streaks of sunlight piercing green walls of pine and laurel, and the buzzing of bees all around him captivated Nikos. Touch and smell, sight and sound, embraced him in concert, infusing him with joy. He wouldn't trade this moment for a thousand others.

Melissa tugged her captive through the rows of thyme toward her bees. As he followed his friend through the thyme, Nikos again marveled at the results of her efforts. Her thyme was among the most fragrant in the region, and her honey brought twice the price of honey harvested by other area beekeepers. Many of them had positioned their hives close to wild thyme, but none had cultivated the herb, systematically selecting only the best to remain close to their hives.

The vibrant young woman pulling Nikos along had done something else. She had planted other flowering herbs and shrubs, watching her bees to see what they liked most, and taking note of when the plants flowered. After a few short years, her bees enjoyed a lavish banquet that lasted from spring's first floral offering until the days grew short and the bees once again disappeared into their hives for the winter.

Melissa had inherited two hives and the cottage from her grandparents. They had brought her up after the *year of dying* took her parents, just as Penelope had raised Nikos after he lost his. It was that shared pain that brought two orphan children together, bonding them in a way that only suffering can.

Now with her right hand still clinging to Nikos behind her and her left one clutching a small ceramic pot, Melissa excitedly skipped to the edge of the clearing. Smoke puffed through a dozen holes in the front hemisphere of the pot, which the young woman customarily brandished to calm her bees. At the moment, though, she seemed oblivious to anything but her present purpose.

Almost as quickly as their short trek began, it ended where the clearing met the northern wall of laurel and pine. The young woman released her friend's hand, spinning toward him as she did. Smoke from the pot formed into a spiral between the two friends, but the swirl rapidly ascended to its own oblivion.

"Do you see anything different?" she asked, flashing a mischievous grin.

Nikos quickly surveyed the row of ceramic pots Melissa had fashioned to serve as homes for her bees. At first he noticed nothing different in this collection of hives sandwiched between the tree wall and the sea of thyme, but suddenly realized the row was nearly twice as long as it had been the last time he stood so close to the bees.

"You've added more hives!" he yelped enthusiastically. "But how did you end up with so many more bees?"

"I split the hives," she replied, her grin partnering with gleaming eyes to convey a playfulness Nikos had seen so many times before. She stopped speaking, as though finished, but he knew she wasn't. Her face was an invitation for him to prod her for the whole story, a story she wanted and needed to share.

"How?" Nikos asked. He had heard her speak of splitting hives before, but had only the dimmest notion of what that meant.

"Do you remember the extra hives I crafted this past winter?" Melissa asked, not stopping long enough for the young man standing before her to do more than nod. "I had to have homes for the new colonies before I could do anything else. After I finished them, I watched."

"Watched what?" Nikos asked, intrigued by her elusiveness. At the same time, he wondered why he had never really paid any attention to this process before.

"The bees, of course!" his auburn-haired friend responded. "The colonies are like creatures themselves. Like hares and pelicans and frogs, they reproduce. That's why bees swarm—to give birth to new colonies! So I watched every day to see when each colony was ready!"

"How would you know?" the young man asked slowly, still in wonder at the idea of a colony of bees being a separate creature.

"When bees want to swarm, they build special places for new queens to be born. Those places are unlike the cells where all the other bees come to life. Whenever I spotted one of these special places, I simply waited for the queen to appear, then loaded her and half the bees from the colony into one of the new hives I built."

"And they stay there?" Nikos asked, surprised that Melissa could so easily move the bees from one hive to another.

Prefacing her answer with a gleeful giggle, the young woman nodded. "I took some of the wax with honey and unborn bees from the old hive and put it into the new one. They've got to protect their babies and their food."

"Will they have enough?" her friend inquired. "For winter, I mean."

"Why don't you decide for yourself," Melissa suggested, quickly stepping up to the hive closest to her. After waving the small ceramic pot around, dispersing smoke to calm the bees, she removed a flat piece of wood from the top of the hive, careful not to crush any of her little friends. She turned around to show Nikos a hanging crescent of wax, full of bees intent on their daily chores. "Here, take it!"

A little reluctant, but also unwilling to show fear, the young man took the wood into his hands. It was heavier than he expected.

"Are all of them like this?" he asked, referring to honeycombs hanging from the flat pieces of wood that lined the top of each ceramic hive. "Are they all full?"

"Not all of them," she replied, "but you'd be surprised how quickly the bees build their comb and fill it," she added eagerly. "These little creatures begin and end their days with the sun. I'm continually surprised by their diligence."

Nikos thought back to his last meeting with Mediocrates and to the garden overgrown with weeds. The old philosopher had insisted that there was very little to be gained from the effort required to remove weeds or to prune excessive growth.

Melissa reached out to take back the honeycomb in Nikos's hands. "It's all I can do to keep up with the bees," she laughed.

The young man realized suddenly that he rarely found Melissa in her cottage. Ever since she had begun working with her bees, she had spent most of her days here, except during the winter. That's when she worked hard to repair tools and to build new hives and other equipment.

"Do you think all this work is worth the effort?" he asked, echoing the question Mediocrates had posed at his garden.

The young woman looked up in surprise. "Of course!" She studied the face of her special friend, hoping to discern his line of thinking. Nikos began to feel uncomfortable.

"It's just," he began. "On my last trip up the mountain—"

"Is that something Mediocrates taught you?" Melissa interrupted. She stood, arms crossed and eyes on fire, like an unyielding guard in some citadel. "How long do you plan to listen to his lies?" she demanded.

Nikos did not respond, but also found it impossible to look directly at his special friend. He was a bit embarrassed.

"Let me tell you," she roared. Nikos was accustomed to her inclination to be blunt, and even passionate, but he was not prepared for the fervor she now displayed. "Or better yet, let my bees tell you! They begin as soon as the sun warms the garden, and they don't stop until the sun disappears. And they won't stop when one comb is full of honey and pollen. When that happens, they build a new one."

The young man finally looked up at Melissa. While she spoke, the exasperation in her voice had gradually evaporated, supplanted by a sense of wonder bordering on reverence. The young woman loved and respected her bees.

Nikos admired many of the traits of his special friend, but no trait inspired greater esteem than her boundless capacity for seeing the extraordinary in the ordinary. He stood speechless, more from a borrowed sense of reverence than from anything else.

"Have you ever realized," Melissa asked in a quiet, reflective voice, "that in good years with plenty of flowers nearby, bees produce far more honey than they will use?"

"I hadn't really thought about it," Nikos admitted quietly.

"It may seem silly to you," she added, once again smiling at the young man who laid claim to so much of her soul, "but I think they do it to share with us."

CHAPTER 13

A LESSON WITH HOLES

Nikos quickened his pace. He needed to make up time because he had run an errand for Penelope early that morning, delivering a cloak she had stayed up late to finish. When she had asked for his help, the young man reminded his mother that he would be meeting Mediocrates. He then pointed out just how warm the weather was and suggested that delivering the cloak the next day would not inconvenience the woman who ordered it.

Penelope, however, insisted that she had promised delivery this day, and that she would deliver it herself, if necessary, to keep her word. At that point, Nikos gave in. As a result, he had begun his trek up the mountain an hour later than usual.

Breathing this morning took more effort, not merely because of the young man's pace, but also because the hot, thick air seemed to resist the efforts of his lungs. On top of trouble breathing, walking was unpleasant. His tunic, dampened by moisture in the air, clung to his body as though it, too, found the heavy air oppressive. Today's climb might not be as perilous as some of his earlier journeys, but it would be every bit as taxing as any of them.

To take his mind off the difficulties of the trail, the solitary hiker began considering the thrust of what he had learned from his mentor. With each lesson, the old man had restated his guiding principle, always referring to it as the *Question*: "Are you willing to throw away all of your todays for a tomorrow that may never come?"

Strangely, the question was both reassuring and troubling. Nikos could not quite determine how the philosopher's question could have two conflicting effects at the same time. At the beginning, he had noticed only the comfort offered by the concept, but later recognized a growing unease. What was it about this question that infused his heart with emptiness?

Grabbing a portion of his tunic with his right hand, the young man wiped his forehead, though the damp garment did little to clear the accumulated perspiration. For a moment, Nikos entertained the idea of turning around, but almost immediately pushed the thought out of his mind. Like Penelope, he had given his word.

"Could it be," the young man wondered out loud, "that by taking tomorrow out of life's plans, the old man's question removes not only anxieties, but also hopes and dreams?"

Nikos stopped abruptly. Long-suppressed doubts surfaced, demanding his consideration.

The young man began walking again, but out of a sense of obligation rather than passion. He had agreed to meet with Mediocrates today, and so he would. As he plodded up the mountain, he paid little attention to his surroundings. Instead, he moved forward much as a defeated soldier, head bowed.

Time passed without his notice until the crude steps fashioned by Mediocrates came into view. Nikos stopped short, bracing himself. His disagreeable teacher sat on the steps. The young man stepped forward, and as he did, the old philosopher looked up. There was no smile, nor was there a warm greeting from teacher to pupil. There was only an antipathy Mediocrates did not attempt to hide.

"I see you've returned," he growled. "What keeps you coming back?"

Nikos froze. "I came for my lesson," he contended with a faltering voice. The young man had been mentally prepared for the dismissive attitude he had encountered before, but not for this animosity. "Did you forget?" He asked, not because he believed the gruff old philosopher had actually forgotten, but because he wanted to avoid conflict. Suggesting Mediocrates forgot their meeting provided an easy excuse.

"Of course not!" The bearded face thrust these words at Nikos as though hurling a javelin in his direction. The old man, clearly in a foul mood, rose to his feet. "How dare you suggest such a limitation in my faculties! Just who do you think you are?"

Pausing to regain his composure, the young man found a renewed confidence as well. "I am your student, I've come for my lesson, and I deserve more respect than you've shown." The words were direct and unabashed, but also without malice or contempt.

This time it was Mediocrates who froze. Cold eyes glared with a ferocity Nikos had not yet seen, but the old man's lips remained still. The two figures stood facing one another, engaged in a war of wills and engulfed in uncomfortable silence. Finally, the philosopher capitulated.

"Yes, I believe you do," he said deliberately and thoughtfully. A disingenuous smile slithered onto the old man's face as he spoke. "And you shall have your lesson," he added, masking threat as concession. "Follow me."

The old philosopher spun around with remarkable agility, his wrinkled robe flustered in its attempt to catch up with its master. Nikos pursued with an apprehensive heart. The old man kept up a vigorous pace down the path, sweeping by the structure with a roof and one complete wall that had been the venue for the lesson involving the broken axe head. Before mentor and pupil reached the hut of rough-hewn logs Mediocrates called home, however, the old philosopher suddenly stopped. Nikos almost ran into him.

"Here." The white-haired, white-bearded man pointed at a shovel lying on the ground next to the path. He said nothing more, but continued pointing.

"Am I supposed to learn something from this?" the young man queried. He looked into the face of his mentor for confirmation. Mediocrates nodded, still pointing.

"Do you want me to pick it up" Nikos asked in frustration. "Or am I supposed to guess why you left a shovel here?"

The old philosopher scowled, then finally spoke. "Start digging. Here, I think!"

The young man looked at his mentor in disbelief, wondering how digging would teach him anything about life or success. Bending over to retrieve the shovel, he picked it up with an exaggerated yank intended to demonstrate his resentment. Mediocrates seemed oblivious. There was nothing left to do but dig.

After breaking through the crusty surface, the young man found the digging became easier. He stole glances from time to time to see whether his mentor was watching, but the old man seemed preoccupied with his own thoughts. Finally, after the hole had consumed Nikos's legs and waist, leaving only his chest and head above ground, Mediocrates spoke.

"This hole is done. Now dig here." He pointed to another spot a few strides from the fresh hole. Nikos wasn't sure, but thought his mentor displayed a smirk, if only briefly.

"Why am I digging these holes?" The young man's words were laced with exasperation.

"Need I remind you *who* is master and *who* is pupil?" The old man spoke with the assumed authority he regularly wore. Nikos reluctantly stepped over to the new location, and after sighing to show his disgust, began digging again. He could already feel blisters developing on the insides of his thumbs and on the palms of his hands.

The young man winced with each movement of the shovel, but continued digging anyway. In and around Pouthena, he had a reputation for hard work. Penelope had taught him that trait, sometimes by vigorously applying her broom to his posterior.

By the time Nikos overtook his mother in height and weight, though, he had come to take pleasure in his work, including physically taxing jobs. He had also learned to use the proper equipment. Unfortunately, he had not anticipated a need for his gloves when he left home for this meeting with Mediocrates.

By the time the second hole matched the first in depth and breadth, the blisters were hindering the young man's progress. Mediocrates pretended not to notice, but couldn't resist issuing another directive to his pupil.

"Stop!" he blurted out. "Put this pile of dirt," he added, pointing to the mound that almost hid Nikos from view, "into that hole." The old man swung around, pointing to the first hole.

"What? Why?" The young man stood motionless. "What's the point?" he demanded, abruptly and even rudely. He was angry now.

"So full of questions, so full...." Mediocrates replied, allowing his words to trail off aimlessly. It was almost as though the old man was thinking out loud rather than answering the infuriated young man waist-deep in the second hole.

The philosopher's subtle grin betrayed his heart to Nikos, who threw the shovel down and climbed out of the hole with a speed that surprised both men. The old man's grin disappeared, replaced by a malicious sneer.

"Answer my question! Now!" the young man insisted.

"Of course," Mediocrates agreed with an ingratiating tone. "But first, perhaps you'll do me the kindness of answering a few of my queries?"

"Ask, then," Nikos growled.

"You came for a lesson today, did you not?" the old man asked, reminding Nikos of his own words just an hour earlier.

"Yes, and I'm still waiting for it!" the young man snapped.

"Have you not noticed how I teach?" The philosopher's plaintive tone was no more genuine than anything else about his demeanor.

Nikos thought for a moment, remembering the old man's often unorthodox approach to teaching. He had, on occasion, used his surroundings, as with the buried axe head and the granite steps. He had even taken a nap to illustrate his principle of waiting for the right moment.

"You use whatever is available," the young man offered in a decidedly unenthusiastic tone.

"Exactly!" the old man exclaimed. "And that's why I had you dig these holes today." He stopped short of a full explanation, crossing his arms smugly.

"And just what do you believe I learned?" Nikos exclaimed, vexed by the philosopher's ways.

"You learned what we all must learn in life – much, perhaps

all, of what others demand is pointless." Mediocrates still wore the sneer Nikos had come to know so well. "If you want to be happy, ignore what the people around you want," he added, with growing intensity. The old man's next words burst from his mouth with a vehemence that caught the young man off guard. "Do what you want! Live life your way!"

With his arms still crossed and his sneer still dominating his face, Mediocrates stood before Nikos as though he had uttered the most profound truth in his treasury.

"So you directed me to dig those holes for no other reason?" the young man asked, knowing the answer before asking. He looked briefly into the old man's face, then at his blistered hands.

"I'm done with you!" he said. "I'm done."

As Nikos turned to head back down the mountain, he could hear Mediocrates chuckling.

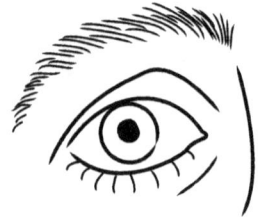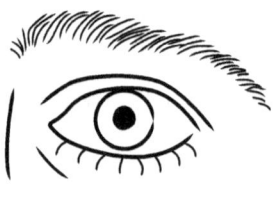

CHAPTER 14

DIFFERENT EYES

Reclining on his back, Nikos reveled in the moment. With his left knee bent to serve as a perch for his right leg, the young man lay in the grass, just as he had so many times during childhood. Unconsciously, he allowed his leg to rock back-and-forth, rhythmically setting a pace for the handful of puffy clouds drifting across a perfectly blue sky. The day was the type that made him glad to be alive.

Lying on a slight incline a dozen paces from the road, Nikos could watch the residents of Pouthena returning to town from their fields, or perhaps heading out of town on errands. Whenever he found himself with a free afternoon on a day such as this one, he often spent it watching. As he lay there, he observed the habits and behavior of his neighbors, all the while considering his own. Through this simple pastime, he had learned much about them, but more about himself.

The young man had been there an hour or more when he heard shouts and curses coming from the other side of a small hill that prevented him from seeing their source. Nikos sat up, hoping he might see something. The sole voice, which had never paused, continued its barrage of some unhappy victim as the top of a head finally came into view. Nikos recognized the voice long before he caught sight of Drakon, a mean-spirited man of about 50.

Nikos already knew who the victim was before he saw him. More than once he had witnessed Lykos walking, head down, as his father uttered one disparaging remark after another. From the few words Nikos could distinguish, this tongue-lashing had something to do with one of the family's goats.

Soon the pair had crested the hill. When they did, Drakon paid no attention to Nikos. Lykos, on the other hand, glanced up, then quickly looked down again in shame as his father heaped insult upon insult on him. In his hand was one end of a short length of rope. The other end was looped around the neck of a goat, presumably the source of the problem.

Although Lykos had never been a friend to Nikos, the young man in the grass couldn't help but pity him. No one deserved that sort of abuse. Unfortunately, no one among Pouthena's residents had ever been able, or willing, to intervene. Nikos didn't think it wise to confront Drakon, but continued watching in hopes of discovering some way to help.

"How someone so stupid could be my son I'll never know!" the furious older man bellowed. His voice was already hoarse from continual roaring, and his face was flushed with rage, but he gave no indication of discontinuing his harangue.

"Adonia!" Spittle flew out of Drakon's mouth as he began a new tirade, this time against his wife. "She's the reason I have such a thick-headed son!"

At this pronouncement, Lykos slumped even closer to the ground, as though hoping to escape into the road itself. There was nothing of admiration or respect, and neither was there anything of joy or peace, in the relationship between father and son.

Drakon spun around unexpectedly, suddenly persuaded of a "truth" he had long suspected. Spewing a flurry of profanities and obscenities toward Lykos, he demanded an answer from the frightened and humiliated young man.

"It's your mother, isn't it? She's the one who's turned you against me!"

Lykos simply stood still, confused and utterly defeated. Unable to reply, he could not even lift his face toward a father who offered only bitterness.

"Don't bother coming home," Drakon declared. "I'll not share my home with a good-for-nothing *son* who conspires against me with his mother!" he added, spewing out *son* as a mark of shame. Grabbing the rope from Lykos, just as he had stolen any sense of dignity from him, Drakon turned his back on the empty young man and marched away, muttering to himself. The goat bleated its own complaints, seemingly echoing the sentiments of its mean-spirited owner.

Drakon disappeared into the distance. Nikos stood, then walked toward Lykos. Frozen in fear, the young man stood in the same spot, head still bowed in shame. A single tear worked to free itself, even as Lykos struggled to draw it back inside. The tear broke free.

When Nikos approached, Lykos turned away, using his left hand to shield a face already swollen and reddened. He braced himself for taunts, but they never came.

"What will you do?"

Nikos's voice was gentle and calm, in stark contrast to the tempest of words that had ended only moments before. Lykos looked up in disbelief. Why should Nikos care? What advantage could he gain by offering comfort? Like an animal with no place to run, Lykos struck first.

"Still dreaming about heroic journeys?" A sneer, long familiar with the lips of this young man, emerged from the shadows of his face. "Wouldn't you be better off working than loafing in the grass like some lazy child? The trouble with you is that you've never had parents to beat the nonsense out of you!" He uttered this last sentence with contempt outwardly directed at Nikos, but in an odd way, also aimed at his father.

For a moment, Nikos stood silent, not sure how to react. Lykos had attacked him without provocation, and yet Nikos could see the pain in the eyes of his enemy. After what he had seen this young man endure, Nikos had no real desire to retaliate. Even so, he saw no way toward peace with such a belligerent young opponent.

Mediocrates would surely describe this confrontational attitude as an *insurmountable obstacle*, advising Nikos to "turn around to avoid aggravation and frustration." Turning and running, though, did not solve the problem, and it certainly did not put him any closer to helping Lykos. But how, exactly, could he help his enemy?

While Nikos wrestled with these thoughts, Lykos glared at him, waiting for the inevitable onslaught. It never came.

"Would you like to have supper with us tonight?" Nikos suddenly asked on impulse, not really sure what to expect.

Lykos stood before him stunned by the invitation. A blow from a fist couldn't have hit him harder. After a few moments, his lips began to move, preparing to utter the type of abuse so routine in his experience. Almost immediately, though, the belligerent young man stopped himself, remembering his desperation.

"I've got nothing better to do," he grumbled, unable to accept the invitation graciously.

This time it was Nikos who was stunned. When he had

extended the dinner invitation, his words were really only something to say to fill the silence. Throughout the years he had known Lykos—years plagued by an unremitting barrage of critical statements—he had never dreamed of inviting the young man to dinner. Rather, his thoughts had always been more about ridding himself and his friends of the company of this unpleasant young man.

"Well then, I guess it's time we start home," Nikos suggested. Surprise quickly turned to dread as the awkward walk began. Neither he nor Lykos was equipped to carry on a conversation with one another. For most of the half-hour journey, the two young men walked in uneasy silence, each immersed in private thoughts and hounded by secret fears.

For Nikos, relief came at the sight of Penelope's little cottage, which had always infused him with quiet joy. He smiled, turning slightly to catch a surreptitious glance at his dinner guest. Lykos wore an impassive face, concealing trepidation and despair.

The quiet travelers left the road, entering the path leading to the cottage. Penelope emerged from the doorway, having spotted the pair through the window.

"How nice to have a visitor!" she exclaimed. "Will you be staying for dinner?"

"Yes, if you please." The words were spoken with a deference Nikos had never heard from the lips of his would-be adversary.

"I'd have it no other way!" Penelope insisted. "Nikos, aren't you forgetting something?" she asked. Her tone was at once pleasant and firm.

"I'm sorry. This is Lykos," he said, sweeping his right arm toward his guest's chest, but keeping his gaze on Penelope's eyes. Her eyes revealed an understanding in her heart. Then, turning to Lykos while gesturing toward her, he continued. "And this is

Penelope, my mother."

"I'm so pleased to meet you," she said with genuine warmth, surprising both Nikos and Lykos, though for different reasons. "And excited to have you stay for dinner."

Turning toward her son, Penelope directed him to show his guest where he could wash up before dinner. Wasting no time, the young man headed to the back of the cottage with Lykos. Nikos reappeared just a few moments later.

"You've mentioned Lykos many times," Penelope said, pausing a moment. "From what you've said, I never imagined you bringing him home for dinner." Her tone suggested she understood much more than she let on.

"I didn't either," Nikos admitted, looking down and shaking his head. "It all happened because I saw his father on another rampage, belittling him without mercy, then telling him not to bother going home. When I tried to offer support, Lykos attacked me!"

Penelope put her hand on Nikos's shoulder, but said nothing.

"I couldn't leave him there," he added, as though defending a poor decision. "No matter what he said to me! The invitation just happened."

Smiling broadly, Penelope took Nikos's face in both hands, turning it toward hers. "I'm really proud of you, son. You acted with the better part of your heart!"

Her hands still held Nikos's face when Lykos reappeared, emotions hidden behind a stony face. At the sight of Penelope and Nikos, however, the young guest's eyes betrayed a melancholy yearning.

Penelope noticed. Letting go of Nikos's face, she briefly squeezed his arm before striding over to her dinner guest. Neither of the young men expected what happened next—Penelope hugged Lykos, and she did so with every bit as much feeling as she always showed Nikos.

At first Lykos pulled back, but Penelope wouldn't let go. She held onto the young man with a determination that could not be resisted. After an awkward moment, Lykos surrendered. Tears came to his eyes, but this time, he didn't seem to care.

"You won't know," Penelope answered, looking directly at Nikos. "You won't always know."

"Why should you take the chance, then?" he asked, confused.

This exchange had begun almost immediately after Lykos left. Having spent the night with Nikos and Penelope, the young man headed out early the next morning. As soon as Lykos was out of earshot, Nikos asked Penelope about the hug she had given their guest.

"He needed it," she explained, offering little else. Dissatisfied, Nikos pressed for more, asking question after question. What made her think Lykos needed a hug? What made her hang on, even as he tried to pull away? And most important, how could she know whether he would respond well?

"You won't know." The words refused to leave him alone. Penelope had acted without knowing how Lykos would respond, but she hugged him anyway. Why? Why take the risk?

"I took the risk because Lykos needed a hug. It's as simple as that."

Penelope watched Nikos closely. "You cannot understand my answer until you have a different perspective," she declared suddenly, sitting up straighter and adopting her usual manner for teaching life lessons. "You must see with *different eyes*!"

Nikos knew what she meant by *different eyes*. As long as he could remember, Penelope had spoken of looking at the world "through the eyes of the people around us." Only then, she insisted, could he begin to understand them.

"I understand that Lykos needed a hug," he spurted out a bit defensively. "What I don't understand is why you would take a risk on someone like him!"

"You did," she said, waiting for him to look back to the incident on the road. "You asked him to dinner. Remember?"

"Yes," he answered, again defensively. "But I don't know why!"

"You should know. You've already told me that you couldn't merely 'leave him there.' Even if you don't know in your head," she added emphatically, "you know in your heart!"

The two sat in silence as Nikos considered all that had happened, though he already knew that Penelope was right.

"Let's talk about the mountain," Penelope suggested as though suddenly inspired. "Let's look at what Mediocrates has taught you."

Anyone else might have wondered about this seemingly impulsive shift in her focus, but Nikos knew Penelope's tactics. When he didn't fully understand her thoughts, she often introduced illustrations from unexpected quarters.

"What was it that the old *philosopher* taught you at the first?" she asked, using a decidedly negative tone for *philosopher*. "It was a question that he presumes the disciples of Hypatos never ask themselves," she added.

"The question," Nikos began, knowing that Penelope did not need to be reminded, "is, 'Are you willing to throw away all of your todays for a tomorrow that may never come?'"

"Does that question satisfy you as a guiding principle?" she asked. Nikos shrugged, but said nothing. Penelope waited, as she always did. The silence was unbearable.

"I think it's a good question," he finally said with no real passion.

"Does it inspire you? Does it motivate you? Does it fill you with zeal?" she asked in rapid succession, already knowing the answer to each question she posed. "Or does it give you an excuse?" Penelope's tone was much sharper in the last question.

Nikos looked down. At the moment, he couldn't look Penelope in the eyes. "I guess it gives me an excuse," he mumbled.

"Would you like to know some questions the disciples of Mediocrates never ask themselves?" she asked, a little playfully. Nikos looked up to see a confident smile.

"Yes, I would!" The words sprang out of his mouth with an enthusiasm that astonished Nikos and gratified Penelope.

"Are you willing to live life without regard for anyone else?" she began. "Are you willing to waste life pleasing only yourself?"

"Just because I don't throw away my todays," Nikos blurted, again on the defensive, "doesn't mean I'm living only for myself!" Even as the words left his mouth, doubt hounded him.

Ignoring her son's assertion, Penelope took a different approach. "Let's take a closer look at the mantra of Mediocrates, shall we?"

Nikos's whole body tensed in anticipation. He had found the old man's principle comforting from the beginning, yet something about the statement had always bothered him. He nodded his assent.

"There are two parts to it. Would you agree?"

"Yes."

"The first speaks of what you do today," Penelope insisted, "and the second looks at how that will affect tomorrow. Do you see anything wrong with my logic?"

"No," was all Nikos said. As a young boy he had learned not to disagree with Penelope unless he had first thought through the issues. She would listen to contentions that made sense, but not to excuses dressed up as ideas. This tenet of Mediocrates, the one that had sidetracked Nikos on his first trek up the mountain, was one he had accepted uncritically.

"Is working for a better tomorrow really a matter of throwing away today?" she asked, looking directly into her son's eyes.

"It could be!" he exclaimed. The intensity of his words reflected a desperation to justify himself.

"I agree," Penelope offered, pausing a moment. Nikos relaxed a little.

"Of course," pausing a moment before continuing. "The mere fact that it *could be*," she added, putting vigor into the last two words of the clause, "means that it also *might not be*."

Nikos said nothing, realizing that she was absolutely right.

"The key, then," the formidable gray-haired woman continued, "is not *whether* you work toward tomorrow, but *how*."

Penelope paused again to study her son's face and posture. In them she saw not only a bit of shame and embarrassment, but also an awakening understanding. She had always believed he would come around, even when he did not believe.

"You must always look to the future," she continued. "Real success is taking pride in knowing that you've done your best today, working not only for today, but for tomorrow."

Nikos nodded, agreeing without reservation, but still embarrassed that he had put so much stock in the guiding principle of Mediocrates.

"There's more," Penelope added, waiting a moment to add gravity to her discourse. The young man looked up, intrigued.

"You must work hard, but never mistake riches, fame, power, and status as measures of success. Yes, it's perfectly acceptable to work toward your own happiness, but never forget the people around you—especially the ones you love!"

Nikos smiled, thinking of all the times Penelope had sacrificed for his happiness.

"Son," she resumed, looking straight into his eyes. "Live today so you won't be ashamed when tomorrow does come. Make no mistake—tomorrow will judge the choices you make today!"

The young man sat there in silence. Penelope was right. And that understanding forced him to reconsider the relationship he had had with Mediocrates. All that the old philosopher had taught was based on living for today.

"One more thing."

Nikos looked up again.

"Do you remember why we began our examination of the mantra of that old pretender?"

The young man thought back, but could not recall the precise reason the conversation had taken this turn. He shook his head.

"I had asked you whether you would be 'willing to live life without regard for anyone else,' and whether you would 'waste life pleasing only yourself.'"

Nikos nodded, waiting for what was coming next.

Penelope smiled, then hugged her son on impulse.

Letting go and stepping back, she declared, "To be successful, you must be humble."

The young man considered her words, but failed to make the connection. "What does humility have to do with success?"

"Everything!"

"But don't you have to be confident to succeed?" he asked. Penelope had always worked hard to instill confidence in her adopted son. Nikos was genuinely baffled.

"One does not hinder the other," she said matter-of-factly. "In fact, someone who is not confident cannot be humble."

The young man's brow furrowed in his attempt to understand. "But to be humble," he protested, "means you don't think very highly of yourself."

"Nikos, my son. Have I not taught you what true humility is?"

The young man shook his head slowly, trying to remember anything Penelope had ever said about the subject. Nothing came to mind.

"Well first, humility is not a matter of thinking you have no value. It's not a matter of denying your talents, or hiding your strengths. It's not really about you at all. Humility is about the *Other*."

"What—or who—is the *Other*?" Nikos asked, even more confused now.

"Everyone else! The *Other* is anyone you're with. The *Other* is your community. The *Other* is your family, your friends, and even your adversaries. The *Other* is Lykos!"

Nikos listened intently, but still did not grasp what his mother meant. "How is that humility?"

"As I explained earlier, humility is not a matter of thinking you have no value. Rather, it's a matter of seeing the value in others. It's not a matter of thinking you have no talents, but of considering how you can use your talents to benefit others."

The young man's eyes brightened and the furrow on his brow disappeared. He was beginning to understand. "Is that why you hugged Lykos, even though you didn't know how he would react?"

"It is. It is indeed," Penelope responded, her face capitulating to a broad smile. "It was humility that prompted me to hug him, but it was confidence that enabled me to act even though I did not know how Lykos would respond."

Nikos smiled.

"Now that you understand, I have a request."

The young man knew the request was more than that. It was an expectation that could not be ignored. "What is it?" he asked respectfully.

"Now that you're done with Mediocrates, I would appreciate it if you would think about all that he taught you in the light of your new understanding of humility."

CHAPTER 15

TO THE TOP

A sea of mist washed up against the mountainside, all the while reflecting reds and golds in the eastern sky. Emerging from his small tent, Nikos paused a moment to appreciate the silent splendor of the morning. As stirred as he was by the beauty of every newborn day, the young man had always felt something more. Daybreak's brilliant light held out promise, speaking to him of the day's potential. This morning, however, that sense of wonder was particularly strong, for today he would finally meet Hypatos.

Almost grudgingly, the young man let go of the moment. He spun away from the east, scanning his campsite to be sure he had missed nothing the day before when he packed his tools into his tent. This spot on the mountain had been his home for weeks as he sawed and planed pine and fir, ultimately assembling them into a new and sturdy bridge. He had built it in the same spot where his primitive bridge once crossed the chasm. Nikos smiled, remembering the pride and the delight he had felt months before as he reached the other side, in spite of the tremendous obstacle in his path.

The idea for erecting a better bridge came to Nikos after Penelope had asked him to reconsider all the teachings of Mediocrates in light of the young man's new understanding of humility. Since that conversation, he frequently found himself slipping away to walk alone in the fields and meadows surrounding Pouthena. He dedicated those walks to rethinking the months spent at the feet of the old philosopher, but also the difficulties of the mountain trail and the experiences in Pouthena after each homecoming. His thoughts turned to his neighbors, and he wondered who among them might decide to climb the mountain. That's when he realized someone needed to build a better, safer bridge. That's when he decided that he should be that someone.

With these thoughts still in his mind, Nikos approached the bridge, filled not only with the delight of having completed a task, but also imbued with joy in having built something that would help friends and neighbors who might follow. The young man strode across the bridge, a bit surprised at how much it pleased him to provide for others.

After reaching the far side of the chasm, Nikos looked back at his creation once more. He had taken time to craft a bridge that was sturdy, but one that also appealed to the eyes. The young man had carefully selected the straightest and best pieces of timber he could find near the chasm. He had studied each piece, considering how it would fit into the construction. He had cut the wood into uniform sizes, planing each piece. And he had built methodically and slowly.

The result inspired him. It was more than functional. That adjective could describe his first bridge, the one he had made by hastily weaving branches together with strips from his fabric girdle and robe. The second bridge, on the other hand, was as much a piece of art as it was a means to cross the gorge.

The young man turned away from the bridge and toward the trail, beginning his trek up the mountain. As he did, he remembered the ugly steps Mediocrates had carved. The old man had insisted that nothing beyond a crude functionality mattered. All goals, according to Nikos's one-time mentor, should be tempered by consideration for personal comfort. Never once did the needs of others come into play.

Nikos shook his head, wondering how such a selfish maxim seemed so appealing to him at the time. Mediocrates had urged the young man never to "set unrealistic goals" and never to "demand too much" of himself. At the time, the advice was unexpectedly comforting, but Nikos now knew why. Declaring a particularly challenging goal unrealistic was a comfortable way to avoid the fear of failure. It was, therefore, an excuse for not trying—and it was entirely selfish.

The trail narrowed. Loose shale on one side demanded Nikos's undivided focus. He chose his steps carefully, bracing for any slippage. The young man negotiated his way through four or five paces before the track once again expanded. As he emerged from this rough patch, the young man remembered his treacherous third journey in the fog. He had nearly fallen off the mountain on that trip—and Mediocrates had not expressed the least bit of concern!

Recalling that his third trip culminated at the home of the old philosopher, Nikos reflected on the disdain Mediocrates had displayed for his collection of scrolls. Even at the time the young man realized that his mentor had to have studied those scrolls, for he knew precisely where he would find the words he needed to illustrate his point. Mediocrates must have spent years in study. Why, then, had the old man grown so hostile to the object of his studies?

Nikos walked in contemplation, but no answer to this riddle presented itself. Why such hostility? What would transform someone's yearning for understanding into a disdain for a life of study? The old man's preference for comfort over exertion would not explain the intense enmity. There had to be a deeper reason.

The young man remembered his own uneasiness at his mentor's animosity toward the scrolls. That uneasiness did not dissipate until his visit with Sophia. Pressing Nikos to look at scrolls as he would people, Sophia had made him realize that scrolls need not be perfect to have value. Furthermore, just as understanding people requires a willingness to step away from assumptions and to consider their viewpoints, understanding scrolls demands a similar willingness to set aside assumptions and an eagerness to consider other perspectives.

Suddenly, the young man had an epiphany. Like Sophia, Mediocrates viewed scrolls as he viewed people, with one big difference. Sophia cherished both, whereas Mediocrates held both in contempt. Nikos realized he would probably never know what disappointments had embittered his one-time teacher, but whatever those disappointments had been, Mediocrates had retreated into his own little world. The old man clearly lived life with regard for no one but himself.

A rabbit shot out from under a bush directly onto the trail in front of Nikos, who nearly tripped himself as he jerked back reflexively. Almost in imitation, the rabbit stopped short, suddenly aware of the much larger creature in his path. Man and rabbit faced each other briefly before the rabbit bolted in another direction.

Nikos watched as the rabbit bounded off, amused at the encounter, but also amazed at the difference a few months had made in his experiences. Months earlier, he had slogged up a lifeless trail. Brown, disfigured trees and bushes all around the mountain seemed lost and hopeless without their leaves. Today, though, the mountain buzzed with life, from the birds to the butterflies—and now this rabbit.

The young man pushed himself forward, still marveling. Everything had seemed so hard that day nearly half a year ago. Rivulets of melting ice had harassed his feet, even as the cold sapped his energy and the darkened skies stole his zeal. When he finally reached Mediocrates, the old man had been surprised, and even annoyed. Only after Nikos had insisted on receiving a lesson did the white-bearded philosopher acquiesce.

Looking back, the young man now knew that what Mediocrates had taught that day was nonsense. Insisting that the best approach to life's most difficult challenges is to wait for the right moment to face them, the grizzled philosopher had never suggested how to recognize that moment. In fact, Nikos wasn't sure there ever was a *right moment* for Mediocrates. In essence, the old man had endorsed an approach to life best labeled as resignation.

At the time, Nikos had been put out with his teacher. He had struggled up the mountain in wretched conditions to meet the old man, only to be received as an intrusion. Mediocrates never acknowledged the young man's efforts, nor did he appreciate his commitment.

Speaking with Andreas had given the young man a new way to look at how to meet challenges, but what really changed his thinking was the exercise Penelope had advised. When Nikos began to consider how waiting for the right moment or of pushing himself would affect the people around him, the picture became quite clear. Mediocrates had waited in his home, comfortably shielded from the freezing rain while Nikos drove himself up the mountain. The old man didn't push himself, but let others do the hard work.

On the other hand, Andreas had pushed himself, all so he could bring in the best fish for his neighbors and friends. The young man shook his head, once more realizing how selfish the old man's philosophy was.

Nikos stopped abruptly. Something was half-buried in the trail right in front of him. The young man knelt down to take a closer look at the small object, and then smiled. He eagerly began to claw the ground around it, exposing more of the item to daylight and confirming his suspicion. It was a *drachma*. What a great find! He dug some more, then yanked the coin from the ground.

Placing the *drachma* into a fold in his robe, the young man stood up to resume his journey. To earn a *drachma* back in Pouthena, Nikos would have spent a day climbing from the harbor to Alexandros's emporium and back again four or five times, all the while loaded with new merchandise. The wage was fair, but when the young man first noticed how Alexandros lived, the wage did not seem to be enough.

He could not argue that the merchant treated him badly. To the contrary, Alexandros always treated him as he would his own son. He expected Nikos to work hard for his pay, but he also took time to teach the young man, just as he had the day he sold the *clepsydra* to Spiros and Xenia. Alexandros had shared something more valuable than a single *drachma* that day. He had shared a perspective on resourcefulness, teaching the young man how to frame his life such that he would be equipped to attack even the most intractable problems.

Nikos smiled, remembering how Mediocrates had insisted

that a broken axe blade was an "insurmountable" impediment to completing a building. Even at the time, the young man had wondered why replacing the axe presented such a barrier, but the question had only enraged his mentor. "How sad," Nikos said to himself, his smile disappearing as he considered how empty and frustrating life had to be for the old philosopher. Surely it was Mediocrates who had been the builder "forced to quit" by circumstances.

As the young man reflected on the lesson of that day, he concluded that it was his teacher who had never considered leaving the mountain to buy a new axe to replace the old one. As a result, the half-finished building stood as a testament to broken dreams and unfulfilled ambitions. And this disappointment was undoubtedly only one among many that had embittered Mediocrates.

What a contrast to Alexandros, who lived with satisfaction in his accomplishments, helping friends and neighbors solve their problems. Mediocrates turned away from "insurmountable obstacles," and in so doing, turned away from the world. Even in this respect, Nikos mused, the old man lived a selfish life.

Glancing to the left, the young man noticed a jumbled mass of wild garlic and cucumbers that brought his hike to a momentary halt as he recognized an opportunity. The morning's hike had made him quite hungry, so Nikos stepped over to the intertwined plants, plucked three of the largest cucumbers, and stuffed two of them into the fold of his robe just below the sash. He wiped the third on the fabric of his robe that covered his belly, and then raised it to his face.

As he bit into the succulent vegetable, the young man thought of Mediocrates, who had been quite proud of spending so little time maintaining his garden. If the old philosopher could see

Nikos now, perhaps he would be envious. After all, the young man had spent *no time* planting or maintaining these cucumbers. That notion brought a smile to the traveler as he resumed his trek up the mountain.

What a difference Melissa's bee yard had been compared to the pathetic garden of his former mentor. He had produced a small patch of garlic, onions, cucumbers, and chick peas, all struggling to survive in a tangle of uncared-for shoots and vines. Melissa, on the other hand, consistently produced both honey and thyme that demanded twice the price of competitors. The old man had disdained work, scoffing at the need to do anything more than get the garden started. Melissa had reveled in working with the bees.

And then there were the bees themselves. As the auburn-haired young woman had pointed out, the little creatures began and ended their days with the sun, producing far more than they needed themselves. Nikos did not really believe, as Melissa had suggested, that the bees persisted in their labors for human benefit, but he did believe that she worked so diligently to produce the best quality for the people of Pouthena.

Yet again the teaching of Mediocrates had proven itself to be self-serving.

Seeing the narrow path ahead, flanked by a sheer cliff wall on the left, Nikos realized he was close to the spot where he had first encountered his former mentor. The young man tensed, recalling the last encounter. That's when the old man had played a malicious trick on his student, pretending that it was a life lesson. As a result of that "lesson" – digging two holes that had no purpose – Nikos had developed painful blisters in both hands, and all his efforts had been for a teacher whose smug demeanor betrayed an unsympathetic heart.

In a way, though, the young man was glad. For several months, nagging doubts about the old man's teachings had lurked in the shadows of his mind. Nikos had refused to examine those doubts because to do so would require him to admit he had been wrong all along. Ironically, it was Mediocrates who had forced his protégé to reconsider. And now, Nikos was free to pursue his original quest. He was on his way to meet Hypatos.

"You again!" a gruff voice bellowed. "I thought I was finally done with you and your dull mind."

The young man turned his head toward the voice, but never stopped walking. Mediocrates stood to the side of the trail, glowering at his former student. Nikos turned his eyes away from the "old scoundrel," as Stefanos had described him. The young man never slackened his pace.

"Where are you going?" This time the words weren't belligerent, but fearful and frantic. Nikos kept walking, even quickening his pace, though he wondered at the old philosopher's fear.

"You'll kill yourself!" These words had gone beyond fear. They were uttered in desperation. "It isn't safe. I tell you, it isn't safe!"

The lonely hiker pushed forward, gripping the rock wall to his left and focusing on the trail before him. As he did, Mediocrates continued to call out, but Nikos ignored the words. He couldn't help but wonder, however, whether the old man's fear and desperation had more to do with his own failures than with the fate of his former pupil.

The cries of desperation slowly faded. Nikos followed the trail around the rock edge, where the trail became wide and level. Yes, today he would meet Hypatos!

APPENDIX I

Guiding Philosophy and Precepts of Mediocrates

GUIDING PHILOSOPHICAL QUESTION:
Are you willing to throw away all of your todays for a tomorrow that may never come?

PRECEPTS GOVERNING SUCCESS:

1. Consider your own comfort when setting goals. Never demand too much of yourself.

2. Don't bother with the advice of others. Do it your way.

3. Don't push too hard for a goal. It'll eventually come to you if it's meant to be.

4. When life places insurmountable obstacles in your way, you're better off turning around.

5. Once you've started a project, relax—allow your project to take care of itself.

6. If you want to be happy, ignore what the people around you want.

APPENDIX 2

Guiding Philosophy and Precepts of Hypatos
(as gleaned from his disciples)

GUIDING PHILOSOPHICAL QUESTION:
Are you willing to live life without regard for others, wasting life by pleasing only yourself?

PRECEPTS GOVERNING SUCCESS:

1. <u>Goals</u>: Consider the needs of others when setting goals. Give the best you have within you, regardless of reward or recognition.

2. <u>Education</u>: Learn as much as you can from others. It is especially important to learn from the *masters* in your field of endeavor, but strive to learn even from the lies you hear, the mistakes you make, and the failures you experience.

3. <u>Drive</u>: Push yourself—no one else will. You'll never get anywhere without moving forward. Drive is especially important in *getting started.*

4. <u>Resourcefulness</u>: First, learn all you can about the world around you. Then, when an obstacle blocks your path, strive to understand the underlying issues. Finally, look for answers from other settings, experimenting with many potential solutions until you find the one that works.

5. <u>Diligence / Perseverance</u>: Keep working, especially when tempted by fatigue to settle for less. Do not allow yourself to be seduced by the idea that you've done enough—there's always more to do!

6. <u>Humility</u>: Value other people, using your talents not only to benefit yourself, but to benefit the people around you. The only real satisfaction in life comes from giving.

APPENDIX 3

Character Roles, Names, and Meanings

I provide this list of characters not so much because they have some deep symbolic meaning, but merely as an insight into my view of their roles in this allegory. I have chosen Greek names, as much as possible, in an effort to infuse Pouthena with a Greek feel. As noted in my introduction, the Western World looks to ancient Greece as the birthplace of philosophy, so suggesting an ancient Greek environment through names seemed logical. In the following list of Greek names, I've provided the more common English derivatives in parentheses, if such exist. I've also supplied meanings when appropriate. Finally, for those characters who teach Nikos about the elements of success, you'll notice key words in bold and italics.

Alexandros *(Alexander)*—the successful merchant. Far too many people in business equate success with the bottom line. Making money trumps the best interests of everyone else, from customer to family members. In my allegory the merchant is wealthy, not because he made riches his goal, but because he chose to use his talent—in this case, ***resourcefulness***—to serve his community. Serving customers rather than taking advantage of them is a lesson learned again and again, often only forgotten by those individuals who inherit thriving businesses.

Andreas *(Andrew)*—the successful fisherman. Success always requires exertion, even when we don't feel like making the effort. People deceive themselves when they think there is an easy path to success. Andreas always had the best catch because of his ***drive***. He and his sons pushed themselves to the limit every day. The Greek name means "manly," which seems quite *apropos* for an individual whose success derives from his sweat. The name also suggests another fisherman who plied his trade on the Sea of Galilee.

Demos—the magistrate. We live and work in a world of rules, some of which we do not like. If we want to be successful, we must learn obedience. This magistrate represents authority as it should be wielded—with uncompromising principle based on understanding and tempered by mercy. He also serves as a father figure, and as such, the perfect sounding board for Nikos as he wrestles with the impact of ***setting life goals*** with no consideration for quality (beauty). The Greek means "the people," and is found in our word *democracy*, a form of government in which the people rule.

Drakon—the mean-spirited father of Lykos. The world is filled with disagreeable people, many of whom rear children in their own image. The Greek means "dragon."

Hypatos—the legendary philosopher at the top of the mountain. He represents the highest aspirations in life. Evidence of the existence of Hypatos can be discerned in the lives of many of Pouthena's residents, but the philosopher himself remains hidden in the book. This hiddenness hints at the elusive nature of life's best choices. The Greek means "highest" or "supreme."

Lykos—the young scoffer who makes himself Nikos's nemesis. Lykos represents the cynicism that so often blocks the positive efforts of other individuals. Caught up in their own miserable view of the world, these bitter souls choose to ridicule us, regardless of whether we strive to "climb the mountain" or choose to settle in as disciples of Mediocrates. The Greek word means "wolf," a pack animal that attacks opportunistically.

Mediocrates—the philosopher dedicated to the middle of the road. Everything about this individual is half-hearted. His philosophy is filled with half truths molded to justify a selfish existence, a life that provides no real joy. The name is an invention for this allegory, though composed of elements of both Greek and Latin. The first half of the name comes from the Latin "medius," meaning middle. The second half (meant to suggest the well-known Athenian philosopher Socrates) comes from the Greek "kratos," which means power.

Melissa—the diligent young beekeeper who has captured the heart of Nikos. Ancient Greek society probably would not have permitted a young woman to pursue her own vocation as a beekeeper. In our story, though, she represents the kind of *diligence*—even tenacity—required for an individual to succeed under the most trying and difficult of circumstances. The Greek name means "bee," a creature renowned for its own dedication to work.

Nikos *(Nicholas)*—the *Everyman* of this parable. In a sense, his story is our story, and we should see in his struggle to succeed what we have experienced in our own lives. Each of us writes his or her own story, sometimes choosing to linger with Mediocrates, but at other times pushing on to a higher goal.

The Greek name means "people's triumph." It comes from the Greek *nike*, which means victory (which is why this word is now a brand of athletic shoes). The name is related to the names Nicholas, Niels, and Nicodemus, all of which mean "people's triumph."

Penelope—the mother figure. Just as Nikos is the *Everyman* of this allegory, Penelope is the *Every Mother*, or ideal mother. She is nurturing, but she never allows her affection to interfere with teaching Nikos what he needs to know. She is self-sacrificing, yet embodies the joy of a life of service. She is the epitome of **humility** as she herself defines it. The Greek name means "weaver," which is why I made her one.

Sophia—the town librarian. This character, like Melissa, is a bit of an anachronism. The ancient Greeks probably would not have entrusted a woman to safeguard its precious collection of scrolls. Sophia, however, is far more than a caretaker. She does not merely respect knowledge, but exudes a passion for **learning** revealed in her references to the scrolls as her friends. Anyone on the path to success must share this passion. The Greek means "wisdom." Combined with the Greek for "love," we have the word *philosophy*.

Spiros—the skeptical customer whose wife Xenia persuades him to visit the emporium of Alexandros on trading day. He is a minor character, but serves as a foil for Alexandros. On the one hand, Alexandros is naturally buoyant and enthusiastic, while Spiros is skeptical and fatalistic. The merchant seeks, and finds, answers everywhere. The out-of-town customer is ready to reject any suggestion that doesn't fit into his narrow world view until confronted with facts he cannot deny.

Stefanos *(Stephen* or *Steven)*—the talented friend of Nikos. Most of us have run into people who are so talented that they coast through life without much effort. Although these people have much to offer, they often fail to push themselves to the limit. How much more could they contribute to the world if they challenged themselves?

Xenia—the villager who drags her husband Spiros to the emporium of Alexandros. Although the Greek name means "hospitality," it is a derivative of *xenos*, which means "foreigner." Since this character is not a resident of Pouthena, but a visitor from an outlying village, the name seems appropriate.

NOTES ON IMPORTANT PLACE NAMES

Daskalos Hill—the location of the Academy. The word "Daskalos" means "teacher," a suitable name for the location of Pouthena's center of learning.

Pouthena—the town at the heart of the allegory. The name is a transliteration of the Greek πουθενά, which means *nowhere*. The idea for this name comes from Samuel Butler's satirical novel *Erewhon*, the title of which is an anagram for *nowhere*.

Claim Your Free Copy!

DISCUSSION PROMPTS:
SIDETRACKED BY MEDIOCRATES

This 15-page PDF is designed especially for youth groups. The questions stimulate discussions about work, success, peer pressure, and many other topics of interest for teens and young adults. Most of the questions require readers to think about their own personalities and character in light of the challenges facing Nikos in the story.

To receive your free copy, email:
littlefrogpublishing@gmail.com

Little Frog PUBLISHING